UPLINK FROM THE UNDERGROUND

Uplink from the Underground

LEFT BEHIND
>THE KIDS<

Jerry B. Jenkins

Tim LaHaye

WITH CHRIS FABRY

TYNDALE KIDS

TYNDALE HOUSE PUBLISHERS, INC.
WHEATON, ILLINOIS

Visit Tyndale's exciting Web site at www.tyndale.com

Discover the latest Left Behind news at www.leftbehind.com

Published in association with the literary agency of Alive Communications, Inc., 7680 Goddard Street, Suite 200, Colorado Springs, CO 80920.

Edited by Curtis H. C. Lundgren

ISBN 0-8423-4318-0, mass paper

Printed in the United States of America

08 07 06 05 04 03 02
9 8 7 6 5 4 3 2 1

To Sara, Caroline, Katy, and Rob

Table of Contents

What's Gone On Before

JUDD Thompson Jr. and the kids of the Young Tribulation Force are living the adventure of a lifetime. After millions disappear, Judd and the others discover they have been left behind.

Judd and Lionel Washington are stranded in Israel when they discover that Judd's friend Nada and her family have been taken into custody by the Global Community. As Judd and Lionel arrive at GC headquarters, the next judgment from God appears. Terrifying horses and riders fly through the streets, spreading deadly smoke and fire. When Judd reaches Nada, a GC guard pulls a gun and threatens them. Nada jumps in front of the man and is shot.

At the hidden schoolhouse in Illinois, Vicki Byrne realizes the horsemen of terror are coming. She hurries the nonbelievers to safety, then confronts the huge horsemen. Finally, after months of praying, former Morale Monitor Melinda Bentley becomes a believer.

With the news that the Global Community is beginning satellite schools, some of the kids disguise themselves and attend the nearest meeting. On the enormous screen, Vicki and Mark watch as true believers are singled out and taken away. Melinda is taken into custody by the Morale Monitors. As Vicki tries to find a seat in the arena, three men in uniform meet her.

Judd grieves Nada's death and is comforted by a letter Nada had written while in prison. With only three months before the Global Community Gala, Mr. Stein decides they should prepare to tell the truth to Potentate Nicolae Carpathia's followers. Judd stumbles across a plan by Nada's brother and father to assassinate Carpathia.

Join the kids as they try to escape the GC's clutches and reach more teenagers with the truth than ever before.

ONE
The Storming Horsemen

As the crowd in the arena wildly applauded, three uniformed men approached Vicki Byrne. One said something into a radio as Vicki concentrated on the screen. She had hoped she was wrong, but it was true. The Morale Monitor outside the arena had nabbed her friend Melinda Bentley.

"We believe there are more Ben-Judah followers inside," the Morale Monitor on the screen said, "and we're going to conduct a thorough search before this session is over. Right now, let's go to Houston, Texas, and find out what's going on there."

The scene switched to a domed stadium, where it appeared other believers were about to be exposed by the GC plot.

Vicki wanted to help Melinda, but she feared the men beside her. One was a GC

Peacekeeper. The other two were younger and wore Morale Monitor uniforms.

Vicki scanned the crowd for a familiar face or someone with the mark of the believer. The auditorium was built in a circle and used for everything from sporting events to rock concerts. She saw no one she recognized. Suddenly, the Peacekeeper grabbed Vicki's arm. "Come with us."

"What did I do?"

Kids nearby turned and shushed them, then stopped when they saw the Peacekeeper.

The man leaned close. "You were running from one of our Morale Monitors. You know the girl we have in custody. Now come quietly or we'll disable you." The man flashed a stun gun.

"Let me get my purse," she said.

The man let go of her for an instant, just long enough for Vicki to break free. She rushed down the row, climbing over legs, stumbling as she stepped on people's shoes.

"We've got a runner!" the man yelled into his radio.

Someone in the crowd shouted, "She's one of the Judah-ites!"

Vicki made it to the end of the row and headed down the steps. Another Morale Monitor came toward her so she turned and headed for the top. Seconds later, another boy in uniform descended toward her.

Vicki spotted a railing and darted into the crowd. Some scooted out of her way while others tried to grab her. She fought to the railing and looked over the side. Too far down. As the men converged on her, she swung her legs over the side and eased down. She took a deep breath and closed her eyes as she prepared to let go.

But a boy grabbed her arm. His T-shirt sported the face of Nicolae Carpathia and the words *The Hope of the World.* "I got her! Help!" he yelled.

Vicki let go of the railing and lunged at the boy with her free hand. She missed, but the boy let go and Vicki fell toward the concrete.

Judd Thompson Jr. knew from reading Tsion Ben-Judah's letters to other believers that the horsemen would kill many more people. Tsion had written that as the world came closer to the forty-second month into the Tribulation, the death toll from the 200 million horsemen would reach a third of the population.

Judd ran back to the patio and joined his friends. He had seen the angry horses before, but never this many. Hundreds and hundreds of thousands stampeded the old city of Jerusalem. The horses had the heads of lions, and fire and smoke poured from their nostrils and mouths. The riders wore gleaming breastplates. Flashes of color nearly blinded Judd, and he had to turn away.

The enormous beasts made no sound as they galloped. It was like a horror movie with the sound muted, but this was scarier than anything Judd had ever seen.

He counted nine people on the street, all unaware of the angels of death ready to strike down anyone God would let them. The people coughed and choked as the smoke billowed around them. All nine fell to their knees and grabbed their throats. One man pulled his shirt over his head in an attempt to block the suffocating smoke. Three collapsed into the gutter and lay motionless.

Mr. Stein knelt and closed his eyes. "I have never seen anything so horrible."

The army of horsemen and their animals kept coming, storming the city in search of more victims. Judd shook his head.

Lionel leaned close. "This makes all the other attacks look like picnics."

"You think this is happening to the kids back in Illinois?"

Lionel frowned. "From what I'm reading off the Internet, this is happening everywhere."

Vicki tried to land on her feet, but she fell backward and smacked the concrete floor, stunning her. When her head hit, it almost knocked her out, but she somehow managed to struggle to her feet. Her legs weren't cooperating, but she realized she hadn't broken or sprained anything. Kids leaned over the railing, pointing and shouting. Two Morale Monitors sprinted down the steps.

Vicki lurched into another hallway and staggered around a corner. She rammed into someone full force, and they both went down.

It was Mark. "Keep going," he said, helping her back up. "I'll stall them."

Vicki raced on, hearing him yell something at the Morale Monitors. As she neared a concession area, she heard footsteps and ducked into a rest room.

Mark Eisman waited until the Morale Monitors were nearly through the tunnel when he stepped out and collided with one of them. "Are you looking for that girl?"

"Yeah, which way?" the Morale Monitor said.

Mark pointed away from Vicki. They turned down the hall, talking into their radios as they ran. Mark looked for Vicki, but she was gone.

He went back inside the arena and noticed a flurry of activity in the stands. Morale Monitors and GC Peacekeepers were searching the stands. A local announcer interrupted the live GC feed on the screen and asked for the cooperation of the crowd. The man described Vicki and asked anyone who saw her to report to the nearest Morale Monitor.

"This girl is a Judah-ite," the man said, "and is dangerous. There is a reward for anyone who helps us arrest her or any other Judah-ite."

The crowd seemed energized. Many looked around while others got up and moved toward the nearest exits.

Suddenly, Mark noticed something strange on the huge video screen. People in Texas were panicking, many running from the domed stadium. The picture switched to a civic center in Memphis, where kids were also running from their seats in terror.

Mark shook his head. Only one thing could scare people that bad.

Vicki found the last stall in the bathroom empty. She quickly swung the door shut behind her and locked it. She took a moment to catch her breath, then looked underneath the stalls. She was alone.

Vicki had to get out of the building without the GC seeing her, but how? Mark or Darrion or Shelly could help, but with thousands of kids in the arena, finding them seemed impossible.

The rest-room door burst open. Vicki held her breath, her heart beating furiously. She sat and raised her feet off the floor. Someone kicked in the first stall door, then the next.

The intruder kicked Vicki's stall door, and when it didn't open jiggled the lock. Vicki saw the standard GC-issue black boots under the door.

She scooted as far back as she could but soon heard what she dreaded. "Global Community Morale Monitor! Unlock this door!"

Vicki opened the stall and a female Morale Monitor stepped inside, closed the door, and locked it.

"You're a Judah-ite," the girl said, "the one we're looking for?"

Vicki studied the girl's face under her uniform cap as footsteps sounded outside.

"Natalie?" someone shouted from the hall.

"In the bathroom!" the girl said.

"Find anything?"

"Nobody," Natalie said. "Had to make a pit stop."

"Get out here. We need your help."

"Why did you do that?" Vicki whispered.

Natalie pushed back her hat, and Vicki saw the mark of the believer. Vicki shuddered. "I thought I was caught."

"You will be if you don't get out of here fast," Natalie said.

"Wait. How did you become a believer?"

"Long story," Natalie said. "No time now."

"The girl being held outside is my friend. We need to help her."

"They've probably already put her in the van. There's no way . . ."

Natalie's voice trailed as screams came from the hallway. Now panicked voices, shouting, and hundreds of kids running.

"Stay here," Natalie said and left.

Moments later she returned. "You're not going to believe this. Come on."

"But they'll see—"

Natalie shook her head. "You're the least of their worries now."

The two made their way through the frightened crowd to the outer ring of the arena. There, Vicki looked through huge windows at a sight she would never forget. Bearing down on them were thousands upon thousands of horses and riders. Hundreds of kids streamed through the smoke- and sulfur-filled hallways, knocking each other down, trampling, coughing, gasping for air, and covering their mouths.

"This is the first I've seen of these things," Natalie whispered. "I read Dr. Ben-Judah's descriptions, but this is worse than I imagined."

Vicki quickly told of her encounter with the horsemen at the schoolhouse. "Remember, the Spirit who lives in you is greater than the spirit who lives in the world."

Natalie nodded. "But what's going to happen to all these people?"

Kids were desperately trying to get outside, but those already out were scrambling to get back inside. "A lot of people are going to die today."

A Morale Monitor raced through the crowd toward Natalie. He raised his gun and fired at the huge window behind them. Glass crashed in the hallway, spreading everywhere. Before Natalie could stop him, the boy jumped through the window and fell to certain death.

Natalie handed Vicki a small key. "Find your friend. This will open the handcuffs."

Vicki gave the girl the address of the kid's Web site, www.theunderground-online.com. "If they discover you or if you want a safe place to stay, write us."

Vicki pushed through the crowd. Kids huddled in corners, screaming and crying. Others had already been trampled to death, their crumpled bodies strewn in the hall like rag dolls. Vicki stepped over bodies, stopping to check for a pulse here and there, soon realizing there was no point.

She spotted the GC truck that had been used for the satellite uplink. A microphone lay on the pavement. The Morale Monitor who had caught Melinda was gone. Mark and Shelly ran up and hugged Vicki. Darrion followed a few moments later.

"I thought they had you," Shelly said.

"Let's get Melinda," Vicki said.

As they walked across the plaza toward the truck, Vicki had to focus. Horses with lions' heads galloped overhead and angry riders bore down on the frightened crowds. Vicki knew she wasn't in danger, but walking close to the thundering herd of demonic beasts was still scary.

Vicki picked up the dented microphone. The truck door was closed, but through a small window she saw an incredible display of video monitors and a huge mixing console. Shelly gave a whoop from the front of the truck, and Vicki and Mark came running.

In the driver's seat sat the Morale Monitor who had shown Melinda on the worldwide satellite feed. Her eyes were open, but she had stopped breathing. Beside her sat Melinda, handcuffed to the passenger-side door handle.

Vicki used the key and quickly freed Melinda. "Let's get out of here."

A huge explosion rocked the plaza. The kids huddled behind the truck and watched the arena fill with flames. Kids scrambled to get out of the way. Some were caught in the blast and killed instantly. Others were trapped inside.

"We have to help them!" Mark yelled over the noise. He ran to the front of the building. Kids screamed and pounded on a huge window, trying to get out. Vicki picked up a heavy rock and threw it as hard as she could, but it didn't even crack the glass.

"Too thick!" Mark said. "I'll be right back." He ran from the area, fumbling in his pocket for something.

Vicki and the others helped as many kids as they could. Some coughed and wheezed, trying to breathe. Others lay motionless.

Moments later Mark raced up in their car. He honked the horn and yelled, "Tell them to move back from the window!"

Vicki motioned for the kids to move back as Mark revved the engine and hurtled toward the building. The crash sent glass flying as kids streamed out, pushing and shoving.

When they had done all they could do, Mark inspected the car. "Flat tire. I'll change it before we head back."

Vicki looked at Melinda. "How did you get here from the schoolhouse?"

"Walked to the main road and hitched a ride."

Vicki frowned. "No way all five of us are getting in this little car."

Mark touched Vicki's shoulder. "I have an idea."

TWO

Lionel's Encounter

"YOU CAN'T be serious," Vicki said, pulling Mark away from the others.

"I'm dead serious. I've had this idea for a long time. This truck could help people learn the truth about God."

"But that thing costs hundreds of thousands of Nicks! It's not right to steal it, even if it's for a good cause."

"We wouldn't be stealing it; we'd borrow it."

Darrion approached and asked what was wrong. Vicki told her.

"I'm with Vick," Darrion said. "The GC will come looking for this."

Mark pointed at the arena. "The GC is reeling from this judgment. They won't be back in operation for at least a couple of days. We can work on my idea in the meantime."

"Tell us," Darrion said.

"I want to break into the GC satellite feed. We wouldn't have much time, but if Carl helped us from Florida, it might work."

Vicki squinted. "You mean, go live to the arena?"

"Not just here, but to every country taking the feed. Think of it! Everybody twenty and under will be at these meetings. If we come up with a creative way to tell the truth, something slick the GC will think is supposed to be there, it could be huge. And with the equipment in the truck, we can record a drop-in and they wouldn't know it's anti-Carpathia until it's too late."

"Didn't you guys do this with a newspaper at your school?" Darrion said.

"Exactly," Mark said. "It'll be the *Underground* by satellite. What do you think?"

Vicki hesitated. "I like the idea. I *don't* like stealing."

"How else are we going to do it?"

"He's got a point," Darrion said. "It's a shame to waste the opportunity."

Vicki pursed her lips. She knew once Mark got an idea, it was difficult to talk him out of it. Vicki recalled the discussions they had had about the militia movement. Judd and Mark's cousin John had advised Mark not to get involved, but he hadn't listened. Vicki wished Judd could help make the decision about the truck.

"I don't feel good about it," Vicki said. "If God wants us to do this, he'll provide—"

"He *is* providing a way!" Mark shouted. "Don't you see? He's put this truck right in front of us, and you're letting it slip through our fingers."

Vicki tried to talk, but Mark cut her off. "Every time Buck Williams writes an article for his Internet magazine, *The Truth*, he's breaking the law. Every time Tsion Ben-Judah writes a letter about Carpathia to believers, he's breaking the law."

"That's different. They're telling the truth, not stealing from the GC."

"Dr. Ben-Judah was a wanted man, and Buck smuggled him out of Israel. Was that right?"

"Of course! Buck saved Tsion's life."

"A lot of people lost their lives today," Mark said. "I want to tell those who are still alive the truth before it's too late."

"I agree. I just don't think God would want us to break one of his commandments so we—"

"Fine," Mark interrupted. "I won't argue theology with the great Vicki Byrne!"

"That's a cheap shot!"

Mark turned and stomped toward the car. He opened the trunk and pulled out the spare tire.

Darrion put a hand on Vicki's shoulder. "Don't let Mark change your mind. Stick with what you know is right."

Lionel watched the final assault of the horsemen with terror and fascination. He knew these were demonic beings, the same as the locusts. But how did they know which people would die? How did the smoke and sulfur and fire kill only people who weren't believers?

Lionel's friend Sam Goldberg logged onto the official Global Community Web site to get the latest official information. "They don't want to admit it, but these horsemen have to be killing a lot of GC personnel."

As the horsemen continued their rampage, Lionel walked alone through the streets near Yitzhak's house. People who had been overcome by the smoke and fumes lay dead in the street. Those who had survived coughed and wandered about, looking for family members. Men and women cried like children. It was a scene his parents wouldn't have let him watch on TV, but now he was living it.

He stood on a corner and watched several Peacekeepers load bodies into a truck. *Where will the GC put all the bodies?* He shuddered and kept walking.

Lionel wanted to be home with the others in the Young Tribulation Force. They had been here in Israel so long. But Mr. Stein's plan of reaching people at Carpathia's Gala interested him. He could wait the three months until that was over to get back to his friends.

As he walked past abandoned cafés and street vendors' booths, he thought about the changes in the nearly three and a half years since the disappearances. He missed his brother and sisters more than he wanted to admit. He had trouble remembering their faces. He had one worn photo of his family left, and he took it from his wallet now and studied it. Clarice had been sixteen when the Rapture happened, the same age as he was now. A wave of guilt swept over him. He had pulled so many pranks on Clarice, everything from messing up her room to lying to boys who called her on the phone. He had once been so mad that he threw her favorite hairbrush in the toilet.

Lionel hadn't treated his little brother and sister, Ronnie and Talia, that bad. In fact, he had hardly paid attention to them. He called them "munchkins." When Ronnie asked him to play basketball or ride bikes, Lionel made up some lame excuse.

Lionel's dad, Charles, had been a heavy-equipment operator in Chicago. He worked long days and was usually exhausted when he got home. Weekends were spent at church, but a few times he'd taken Lionel to a White Sox game.

Thoughts of his family came back at different times. Sunday mornings were hard. Lionel remembered the drive into the city, the stop at the donut shop where the kids would pick out their favorites. Birthdays at his house had been a huge deal, with cakes and presents, parties, and friends. His mom had always organized the fun. She had a way of knowing exactly what Lionel wanted, even without asking him. It was almost like she could crawl inside his mind. He would come home from a bad day at school and try to keep it inside.

But when his mom got home from her job at *Global Weekly*, all it took was one look. "What's wrong?" she would say, and he would spill it all. Of all the people on earth, he missed his mother the most.

On the morning of the disappearances,

Lionel had been with his uncle André. It didn't take Lionel long to figure out what had happened. Unlike others who didn't have a clue, he knew exactly where his family was. Sitting next to his father's bedclothes, watching the horrifying news on television, he had felt so alone. Why couldn't he have been taken to heaven? But he knew the answer. He had never begun a relationship with God. He had played the good Christian, and everyone bought it. Everyone but God.

Now, as Lionel walked through the burning streets of Jerusalem, he knew there were many others just like him. They had either played at church, or they believed there was some way to God other than through Jesus.

Lionel found himself quite a distance from Yitzhak's house. He turned to retrace his steps, but stopped when he saw part of the city with no smoke or fire. He was near the Wailing Wall. A few steps farther and he saw Eli and Moishe, the two prophets of God.

Vicki and the others waited while Mark changed the tire. They could barely see through the smoke and fire near the arena. It billowed black and yellow.

"Will these things disappear like the locusts?" Shelly said.

Vicki shrugged. "I guess they'll leave when they're supposed to."

Melinda watched for any sign of GC Peacekeepers. Most had run away or had been killed. A few walked through the crowds, coughing and sputtering.

Vicki took Melinda aside. "I thought we made it clear you would stay at the schoolhouse."

"I know," Melinda said, "but I was so excited—"

"I understand, but you're not just living for yourself now. You're part of a group. What you do or don't do affects everyone."

"I didn't think about getting you guys into trouble."

Mark finished with the tire and handed Shelly the keys. "There's not enough room for all of us. You guys head back."

"We're not leaving without you," Vicki said.

"Yes, you are. I'll find another way."

"No!" Melinda said. "This is my fault."

Mark held up a hand. "I've made up my mind. I'll see you guys back at the schoolhouse."

Vicki nodded and all four girls climbed inside the little car. As Shelly drove away,

Vicki noticed Mark walking into a thick cloud of smoke.

"How's he getting back?" Darrion said.

"He'll find a way."

Lionel walked slowly toward the two witnesses. They still wore sackcloth robes and looked like the picture of John the Baptist in Lionel's first Bible. They had dark, leathery skin, and their feet were dirty. Their bony hands stuck out of their clothes like sticks, and their long gray hair and beards floated in the breeze.

Each time Lionel had seen the two witnesses in televised reports, there were crowds of curious onlookers and GC guards nearby. Now there were only dead bodies near them.

Lionel wondered if the two would notice him. If they did, would they speak to him?

Eli turned his head slightly and said, "Oh, taste and see that the Lord is good; blessed is the man who trusts in him!"

Moishe, without moving his lips, raised his voice. "The eyes of the Lord are on the righteous, and his ears are open to their cry. The face of the Lord is against those who do evil, to cut off the remembrance of them from the earth."

Eli stood and motioned for Lionel to come further. " 'The righteous cry out, and the Lord hears, and delivers them out of all their troubles. The Lord is near to those who have a broken heart.' "

Lionel thought of Judd and Nada's family. Could these two prophets of God be giving him a message for them?

"Comfort one another with these words," Moishe said.

Lionel sighed and inched closer. "If you'll permit me to ask a question?"

The two stared past Lionel. Finally, Eli moved his head a few inches.

"I know the Bible says you're going to prophesy for a set time. What happens after that?"

Eli and Moishe spoke together. "As it is written, 'And I will give power to my two witnesses, and they will prophesy one thousand two hundred and sixty days.' "

" 'When they finish their testimony,' " Eli said alone, " 'the beast that ascends out of the bottomless pit will make war against them, overcome them, and kill them.' "

The two witnesses fell silent, with sad looks on their faces. Finally, Moishe said, "Take heed. The god of this world seeks the death of those who follow the true and living

God. Be wise as serpents and harmless as doves."

"The beginning and ending are written in the book," Eli said. "Be diligent to present yourself approved to God, a worker who does not need to be ashamed, rightly dividing the word of truth."

Eli and Moishe sat. Lionel could tell his time was up. He didn't know what to do, so he bowed, said thank you, and left.

As Lionel walked to Yitzhak's house, he thought about Eli's and Moishe's faithfulness to God. He slipped inside the house unnoticed and looked up the first news report about the witnesses. Carefully counting the number of days, Lionel calculated when the 1,260th day would be. He studied a calendar and gasped.

Mark Eisman watched Vicki and the others drive away. He climbed a brick wall near the arena to survey the area. Bodies littered the plaza and fire licked at buildings. A gas station a few blocks away was nothing but a hole in the ground.

Mark walked back into the arena. The screen was blank and the auditorium empty, except for dead bodies. Through a window he noticed the satellite truck. He ran outside, keeping watch for Peacekeepers or Morale Monitors, and climbed behind the wheel.

He picked up a cell phone on the seat and punched a few numbers. After several rings a man answered and said, "Satcom headquarters."

"Carl Meninger, stat!" Mark said.

Vicki and the others were exhausted when they pulled up to the schoolhouse. Lenore made them all sit and tell what had happened while she made dinner.

Charlie stood. "What's that rumbling?"

Vicki went to the window. A cloud of dust rose from the secret entrance to the hideout.

Janie rushed into the kitchen. "Is it the smoke and fire again?"

"I don't think so," Vicki said. She ran outside and gasped as a satellite truck pulled in front of the schoolhouse.

Conrad gave a low whistle. "Cool."

Vicki shook her head. "Not cool."

Mark jumped out. "I know what you're thinking. Just hear me out."

Vicki crossed her arms. "We agreed we weren't going to steal GC property."

"That's the good news. This truck doesn't

even exist. Carl got into the computer at headquarters. This thing was destroyed in the attack."

"How could it be destroyed if we have it?" Charlie said.

"They'll never look for it," Mark said.

Conrad ran to the back of the truck and opened the door. "Hey, guys, come see this!"

"We know," Vicki said. "The latest technology and—"

"No," Conrad said, glancing at Mark. "Didn't you inspect this?"

"Inspect it for what?"

Conrad opened both doors. The truck was filled with video monitors and complex electronic equipment. On the floor lay someone dressed in a Morale Monitor's uniform.

Conrad looked at Vicki. "She's still alive."

THREE

The Sleeping Enemy

VICKI stared at the girl and shook her head. She couldn't believe Mark had endangered them this way.

Mark put his hands in the air. "I didn't know she was here. Honestly, I'd never—"

"Doesn't matter now," Vicki said. "Let's get her inside."

Conrad and Mark carried the girl upstairs and gently placed her on a cot. Lenore brought medical supplies.

"I know this girl," Vicki said. "She's Marjorie something, the one who checked me into the arena."

Lenore turned her name tag over. "Her last name is Amherst."

Vicki nodded. "She was the valedictorian at Judd's graduation."

"She's in bad shape," Lenore said. "I'll

work on her while you decide what to do if she wakes up."

Vicki went downstairs and found Mark explaining his idea. Their friend Carl was preparing to uplink the kids on the GC satellite.

"How's Marjorie?" Melinda said.

Vicki gave them an update and told them who she was. Mark remembered her and said they had taken a couple of classes together. "She was always blowing the grading curve because she got such high scores. Everybody hated and admired her at the same time."

"How could somebody so smart fall for Carpathia's lies?" Charlie said.

"The Bible says people will never find God through human wisdom," Vicki said. "When we talk about Jesus dying for them, they think it's foolish."

"You mean, you can't be smart and believe in God?" Charlie said.

"No. Look at Tsion Ben-Judah or Buck Williams. They're really smart." Vicki picked up a Bible and turned to 1 Corinthians. "God picks things we wouldn't pick to show how great he is. He chose David even though he was a shepherd. He chose Jesus to be born in a stable to very poor parents."

"So God does things backwards to the way we'd do them?" Charlie said.

"Yeah, in a lot of ways. Listen to this: 'God deliberately chose things the world considers foolish in order to shame those who think they are wise. And he chose those who are powerless to shame those who are powerful. God chose things despised by the world, things counted as nothing at all, and used them to bring to nothing what the world considers important, so that no one can ever boast in the presence of God.' "

"I get it," Charlie said. "People with a lot of brains can follow God as long as they understand God is smarter than their smartest ideas."

The kids smiled and Vicki chuckled. "And it also means you can use all kinds of arguments, but people have to realize they have a problem only God can fix."

"Sin," Mark said.

"I thought I was pretty smart," Darrion said. "When Ryan talked about God, I thought he was nuts. Somehow, God showed me I needed forgiveness."

"Which brings us to Marjorie," Vicki said.

Melinda frowned. "Sounds like she's really into the GC."

"This is my fault," Mark said. "If she recovers, we'll blindfold her and I'll drive her back in the satellite truck."

"The one that doesn't exist?" Vicki said. "That'll tip off the GC, and we'll get Carl in trouble."

"All right, I'll take her in the car."

"Wait," Melinda said. "Is that all we're going to do with her, just ship her back? You didn't do that with me. You guys were straight with me from the start."

"That's because you were holding a gun," Mark said.

"I think you would have told me the truth even if I hadn't been."

"She's right," Vicki said. "I don't want to pretend. We shoot straight with Marjorie, and if she wants to go back to the GC, we'll take her."

"She might still be able to lead them to us," Mark said.

"True, but she might also believe what we tell her," Vicki said.

Lionel couldn't wait to tell about his meeting with Eli and Moishe, but he especially wanted to talk with Judd. He found everyone downstairs in Yitzhak's house with a new group of witnesses. Lionel described the meeting with Eli and Moishe, then pulled out a piece of paper.

"I've counted up the 1,260 days since Eli and Moishe first appeared. If I'm right, their final day will come during Carpathia's big celebration."

"That's in less than three months," Judd said.

Mr. Stein shook his head. "Perhaps that is the reason for the party. Carpathia will snuff out these precious lives, and everyone will praise him for ending the judgments."

"They're really just beginning," Lionel said.

A tall man with huge shoulders stood. He wore tattered clothing like Eli and Moishe, and spoke with a thick European accent.

"God has given us a wonderful tool in the Scriptures," the man said. "We can read history ahead of time if we look to the Bible."

"What's going to happen to the two prophets?" Sam said.

"Tsion Ben-Judah has written much about our friends at the Wailing Wall. If you examine the Bible, you see that God has given them power to pronounce judgment on his behalf."

The man continued. "But their mission will end. The Bible says that one day they will complete their testimony, and the beast of this world will kill them. And their bodies will lie in the main street of Jerusalem."

"I don't want those guys to die," Sam said. "We have to save them."

"Everything has a purpose in the plan of God. After they die, no one will be allowed to bury them. People from all over the world will come to look at their bodies and celebrate. The people will even give presents to each other as they rejoice in the deaths of these two prophets."

"How will Carpathia kill them?" Judd said.

"I'm not sure, but our friends will not stay dead. God will raise them to life."

"I want to see that," Sam said. "And I want to see the look on Carpathia's face when it happens."

Lionel motioned for Judd and called Nada's family together. "I think Eli and Moishe gave me a message for you."

"What do you mean?" Kasim said.

"Both of them quoted verses from the Psalms. They talked about God hearing the cries of the righteous. They said God's against those who do evil. And then they called me closer. The way Eli looked at me . . ." Lionel felt the tears coming as he looked at Nada's mother.

"What did he say?" Lina said.

"I printed it. It's from Psalm 34." Lionel's hands trembled as he read. "'The righteous cry out, and the Lord hears, and delivers them out of all their troubles. The Lord is near to those who have a broken heart; he rescues those who are crushed in spirit.'"

When Lionel looked up, Nada's parents were crying. Kasim looked at the floor. "One of the last things Moishe said was 'Comfort one another with these words.'"

Jamal wiped his eyes. "We've known God cares about our loss, but these words help more than you can know. Thank you."

Vicki took turns with the others watching Marjorie. Lenore had taken the girl's pulse and blood pressure every hour, but there was no change. Vicki volunteered to stay with her through the night.

Lenore gave Marjorie's walkie-talkie to Mark. Her empty gun was on the nightstand alongside a radio. Vicki tuned in a GC station to get the latest news.

The announcer seemed shaken by the numbers of dead or missing. "Experts fear fatalities may go higher. Global Community officials have no further word on the cause of the plague of fire and smoke. Potentate Nicolae Carpathia will address the world from New Babylon tomorrow."

Mark laid the walkie-talkie on the nightstand. "It doesn't have a homing device. I removed the solar cell so she can't communicate with headquarters."

Vicki followed Mark into the hall and told him about the Carpathia address. Mark turned. "I'm really sorry about bringing her here."

Vicki smiled. "I've made a lot of bad decisions since I became a believer. But I do believe God even uses our mistakes."

"What do you want to do with the truck?"

"Let's see what happens with Marjorie. I like your idea about breaking into the satellite school signal, but I don't have any idea how you would do it."

"I talked with Carl for a long time tonight. We're getting a plan together. You know the believers who were singled out in the meetings?"

"I can't get them out of my head."

"Carl says only a few were taken into custody. Most got away when the horses attacked. He told me what it was like watching those horses come in over the Atlantic."

"Scary, I'll bet."

"Yeah. The GC picked up a cloud on radar that stretched from Florida to Maine. Carl got into one of the observation towers and said he could see millions of horses coming over the water."

Vicki shuddered. "And it happened all over the world at about the same time."

"Yeah. Carl said the horses killed a lot of the GC communications team. He's one of the higher ranking officers now."

"Tough way to get a promotion."

"The interesting thing is what happened when the horses left. Carl saw them from the observation deck running toward the water. Millions of horses passed him and instead of running on top of the water, the horses and riders dove straight down and disappeared."

"So it's over?" Vicki said.

"Sounds like it to me."

"What's the next judgment?"

Mark squinted and looked past Vicki.

"What?"

"I thought I saw something move."

Vicki turned and walked into the room. Marjorie lay still, her eyes closed. Vicki took the girl's wrist to check her pulse.

Marjorie opened her eyes and grabbed Vicki's arm. With her other hand she snatched the gun from the nightstand and pointed it at Vicki. The girl sneered at Mark. "Come inside and close the door, Judah-ite!"

girls who lived [illegible]. And they moved all over the world at about the same time.

[illegible] the house [illegible] [illegible] [illegible] are [illegible] officers now.

[illegible] near to get a promotion.

[illegible] things what happened [illegible]

[illegible]

[illegible] moved [illegible] and wandered [illegible]

[illegible]

FOUR

Deadly Plans

VICKI backed away as Marjorie released her arm and rolled out of bed. When the girl's feet hit the floor, she wobbled and nearly fell. She tried to keep the gun steady. "Get inside and close the door. I don't want to have to kill anyone else."

Vicki looked at Mark. He stepped inside and closed the door. "How long have you been awake?" Vicki said.

Marjorie coughed. "Long enough to know you guys aren't followers of Potentate Carpathia. How did I get here?"

"We found you in the back of the satellite truck outside the arena," Mark said.

Marjorie put a hand on the wall to steady herself. "I remember the smoke and that awful smell. I ran for the truck because . . ." She looked up. "You kidnapped me!"

"We didn't know you were inside."

Marjorie moved gingerly to the window and glanced outside. "You stole it?"

"It's a long story, but—"

"Where are we?"

Vicki stepped forward. "Sit down. You look woozy."

"Stand back. I don't need your help." Marjorie grabbed the walkie-talkie and clicked the microphone. "Morale Monitor Marjorie Amherst. I'm being held hostage. Over."

Marjorie clicked the radio again but there was no answer. She threw it in the corner. "Smoke probably ruined it. Tell me where I am."

Vicki decided there was no reason to make up a complicated story Marjorie wouldn't believe. "You're right. We're followers of Jesus Christ."

"Ben-Judah, you mean."

"He's one of our teachers, yes."

Marjorie studied the moonlit woods surrounding the schoolhouse. "What is this place, a Ben-Judah training camp?"

Vicki smiled. "Not a bad guess. We moved into this abandoned building after I had a dream about it."

Marjorie squinted. "You *are* crazy."

"I know it sounds weird, but it's true. There are a bunch of us living here. When the locusts came, we took in a lot of people and tried to help. We did the same when the horses and riders started—"

Marjorie shook her head. "I'm not buying the horse story. It's a trick. Somebody's been releasing poisonous gas and setting fires. You Judah-ites are the main suspects."

"Why?" Vicki said.

"Have you seen any Judah-ites getting sick or dying? You know exactly when and where things are going to happen, like at the arena yesterday."

Mark rolled his eyes. "You were there. Did you see anyone setting fires or releasing poison? God's the one letting this happen."

"Right. It was God who let my parents and most of my friends get killed. It was God who killed our principal at Nicolae High. Mrs. Jenness was one of my best friends. . . ."

Marjorie sat on the bed. Vicki stepped closer, but the girl looked up and waved the gun again. "Stay away."

"We want to help you. If you'll let us explain, I think it'll all make sense," Vicki said.

Before Marjorie could speak, the door opened and Lenore peeked inside. She gasped when she saw Marjorie.

"Get in here! Now!" Marjorie shouted.

Vicki waved Lenore inside. "It's okay. She can't hurt us."

"What do you mean? I'll shoot all of you."

"How long has she been awake?" Lenore said.

"Not long," Vicki said as she stepped closer to Marjorie and reached for the gun.

Marjorie scampered back onto the bed, her hands shaking. "I swear I'll shoot."

Vicki held up her hands. "We don't want to hurt you. We just want you to know the truth."

"Don't say I didn't warn you." Marjorie pointed the gun at Vicki's knee and pulled the trigger. *Click. Click. Click.* "You tricked me!"

Judd watched the reports of death on the Global Community News Network. Reports from around the world were grim. The GC braced for yet another mysterious "attack," as they called it, but Judd and the others at Yitzhak's house believed the horsemen were gone.

Judd decided to come up with a creative way to publicize Mr. Stein's meetings during the GC Gala. Judd was glad to get his mind off Nada's death and Jamal and Kasim's plan to kill Nicolae. He went to Mr. Stein and suggested they print pamphlets and let witnesses pass them out in Jerusalem.

"Wonderful," Mr. Stein said. "Now I have news. I have met with Yitzhak and some of the other believers, and we believe we should not wait. We want to begin these meetings now."

"Why now?"

"People are struggling with the deaths of loved ones. They need the hope we can offer."

"What about during the Gala?"

"We're still planning it, but we think God wants us to get the message out now."

Yitzhak gave Judd directions to a print shop owned by a believer. As Judd walked, he felt he was being followed. He quickly ducked into an alley. Moments later, Kasim ran past and Judd grabbed him. "Why are you following me?"

Kasim pulled Judd deeper into the alley. He caught his breath and said, "I didn't want to talk to you at the house. I've made up my mind to assassinate Carpathia on the first night of the Gala."

"That'll put a cloud over the celebration," Judd smirked.

"Yes, but it also means Eli and Moishe might have more time."

Judd shook his head. "You know it doesn't work that way. The Bible says—"

"Your interpretation is different from

mine. If I can get to Carpathia, it could change everything."

"It's clear that Eli and Moishe—"

"What happens in the future happens. I can only do my part and rid the world of this evil man."

Judd sighed. "Okay. I don't agree with you, but I made a promise not to tell anyone about this."

"I don't want you just to keep quiet. You must help. I have a diagram of the buildings near where the stage will be built."

"No way! This idea belongs to you and your dad."

Kasim looked away. "My father is not willing to help any longer. That's why I need you."

"What changed his mind?"

"It may have been the words of Eli and Moishe that Lionel shared. Or perhaps my mother persuaded him to give up the idea."

"Has he tried to talk you out of it?"

Kasim looked away.

Judd grabbed Kasim's arm. "Listen to him. Forget your revenge on Carpathia. Use your energy for something more important. There are people who might come to know God if we can reach them with the message." Judd pulled out the file he had worked on for Mr. Stein. "We can reach so many people if you'll help. That's the real way to get back at God's enemy. Steal people who would otherwise choose Carpathia."

Kasim leaned against the brick wall and slid to the ground. "You don't understand. I wake up at night sweating, planning Carpathia's demise. It's all I can think about. I pledged my life to this monster before I understood the truth. I don't want anyone to make that same mistake."

"I understand that, and I know how much you loved Nada and how bad you feel about what happened. But the truth is, even with Carpathia dead, his evil will continue. The prophecy is clear—"

"Nothing you say will keep me from this. The only question is whether or not you will help me."

Vicki didn't want to lock Marjorie in the basement hideout, but the kids couldn't let her get away. Vicki made sure Marjorie didn't see the door to the underground tunnel and that there was enough food and water for the night.

The next day, Mark brought Marjorie to the computer room, where Lenore and Vicki were waiting. Everyone else stayed out of sight so they couldn't be identified later.

"The GC are probably looking for me right now," Marjorie said.

"We want to do the right thing," Vicki said. "We'll take you back if that's what you want, but we need a little time."

"I can't stay here. The satellite schools—"

"It'll take a few days to get everything running," Mark said. "I've been watching the news." Mark turned on the monitor in time to see the introduction to the live broadcast of Nicolae Carpathia.

Vicki leaned close to Marjorie. "What we'd like you to do—"

"Wait. I want to hear this. Turn it up."

Mark turned up the audio as Nicolae began. He expressed his sorrow for the families of victims who had died in the past few months.

"My advisors inform me that more people have died in this most recent wave of deaths than those who disappeared nearly three and a half years ago. That means there will be perhaps as many as a billion who have passed away since the beginning of the smoke, sulfur, and fire.

"There is no one on the planet who has not been touched in some way by this destruction. And it is my goal to end the suffering."

The camera zoomed in on Carpathia. He looked down, bit his lip, and gave a slight nod. "My advisors also inform me there is reason to believe this disaster was not a natural phenomenon. The earthquake and the fiery meteors were clearly explainable events, but this chemical warfare and arson are part of a calculated plot by the enemies of peace."

"That's what you guys are!" Marjorie yelled.

"This guy has never wanted peace," Mark said.

"Just wait, he'll show you."

"I am asking anyone who has knowledge of those responsible for these deaths to go to your local Global Community authorities. Any tip or lead that exposes those responsible will be rewarded."

Nicolae outlined a plan to dispose of the bodies. "Of course, many have already been destroyed by fire, but in order to keep our world healthy and free of disease, I have ordered our ministers of health to arrange mass burnings throughout the world. This will not be a pleasant task for loved ones or for the officials charged with this duty, but it is something that must occur."

Vicki thought of the grisly job of burning the dead. Who would they hire to do such a thing? Vicki shuddered and tried to concentrate on Carpathia.

"I have plans for at least two of our enemies, and those plans will be carried out at the Gala in Jerusalem. It is time for us to put the death and grieving aside. And so I invite you, wherever you are, to this grand party. Even those who are against our ideals should come. To show how accepting and tolerant I am, I extend a personal invitation to Rabbi Tsion Ben-Judah. He may attend our celebration as an international statesman."

"That shows you what kind of man the potentate is," Marjorie said. "He even invites his enemies."

The camera pulled back as Carpathia walked to the front of his massive desk. "We have every reason to want revenge, but as your leader and a man committed to peace, I offer one more opportunity to our enemies. Let us put aside our differences and strive together for a new world of love and unity. Join the faith of your brothers and sisters across the planet, the Enigma Babylon One World Faith."

Mark shook his head as Carpathia finished. "That doesn't make sense. Those people at the satellite school were determined to catch followers of Ben-Judah. Now Nicolae's giving us a free ticket to his party?"

Vicki faced Marjorie. "There's one condition to taking you back. You have to listen to the truth."

"I just heard the truth. Potentate Carpathia *is* the truth."

Janie opened the door and walked in. "I didn't know you guys were in here. I heard there was a Morale Monitor in the house, but—"

Marjorie studied Janie's face. "Do I know you? You look familiar."

"I'm sure we haven't met." Janie asked if she could stay, and Vicki said it was okay.

Vicki turned to Marjorie. "Let me explain what we believe before you leave. After you hear me out, if you still want to go back, we'll work it out."

Janie sat down, rolled her eyes, and muttered, "Don't waste your breath."

Marjorie sat up. "Now I remember. I saw a poster with your picture. You were in a reeducation facility downstate."

Janie shifted in her chair. "That's crazy. I don't know what you're talking about."

Marjorie looked at Vicki. "I'll listen on one condition."

"What's that?"

"If I listen to you, you have to listen to what I think about the Global Community."

"Deal."

FIVE

Vicki's Surprise

VICKI asked Marjorie what she thought had happened to those who had disappeared three years earlier. Marjorie gave the same answer as Global Community scientists. Their theory didn't make much sense, but Vicki didn't challenge it.

"And what do *you* think happened?" Marjorie said.

"I think the Bible came true before our eyes."

Marjorie rolled her eyes. "Oh yeah, God came back and took all the good people to heaven and left the bad ones. What does that say about you?"

"The people who disappeared weren't perfect. They had a relationship with God."

"Which means that my mom and dad, who were really good people, came up on the short end?"

"I'm not criticizing your parents or you. I'm telling you what happened. Did you have any brothers or sisters?"

"I'm an only child."

"Figures," Janie muttered.

Vicki gave Janie a look, then explained what had happened to her family. "The same thing happened to most of us here. One girl actually saw her mom disappear, and right before she did, her mom told her exactly what I'm about to tell you."

"I can hardly wait."

Vicki told the truth as simply and clearly as she could. Marjorie smirked when Vicki quoted Bible verses, but Vicki knew God's word had the power to change a person's heart.

"In Romans it says, 'For all have sinned; all fall short of God's glorious standard.' But it doesn't stop there. God loved us enough to give himself and pay the penalty for our sin. Then it says, 'Yet now God in his gracious kindness declares us not guilty. He has done this through Christ Jesus, who has freed us by taking away our sins. For God sent Jesus to take the punishment for our sins and to satisfy God's anger against us. We are made right with God when we believe that Jesus shed his blood, sacrificing his life for us.' "

Marjorie yawned.

"Another verse says that the punishment for sin is death, which means we'll be separated from God forever."

"That doesn't seem fair. I only do one bad thing and I get the death penalty?"

Vicki explained God's holiness. "Say you have a gorgeous new Morale Monitor uniform. You've just shined all the buttons, you have a pair of bright white gloves on, and then you find out somebody has worn your boots and walked through mud."

"I'd be ticked."

"Would you wear the boots?"

"Of course not. I'd shine 'em up."

"Right," Vicki said. "Now think about God. Every part of him is perfect. Would you expect him to allow anything in his presence that's not perfect?"

"I guess not. But that would mean we're all doomed."

"Exactly, but stick with me. God knew we were all imperfect. He knew we'd do bad stuff, and that even one sin is enough to separate us from him forever."

Marjorie made a face. "I still say it's not fair. Why couldn't we have one more chance?"

"God did better than give us another chance. He took the sentence himself."

Vicki showed Marjorie different parts of

the Gospels. She quoted John the Baptist, who looked at Jesus and said, "Look! There is the Lamb of God who takes away the sin of the world!" She told her about the miracles Jesus performed, that he lived a perfect life, and was finally crucified.

"If he didn't do anything wrong, why was he put to death?"

"Most of the religious leaders of the day hated Jesus because he said he was God. They handed him over to the secular leaders to kill him. But the truth is, Jesus let himself be killed. That's what the Bible means when it says God sent Jesus to take our punishment."

Marjorie hesitated. "I guess some of it makes sense, but if I have to choose between your religion and Potentate Carpathia, I'm going with the GC."

"Jesus said anybody who isn't for him is against him."

"Carpathia thinks Jesus was a great man."

Vicki shook her head. "That's not an option. Jesus said he was the only way to God. He claimed to *be* God. If that's not true, he's either a fake or he's crazy. Would you call someone who's lying or loony a great moral teacher?"

"I guess not."

"Then there's only one other option. Jesus is God."

Marjorie walked to the window. "I'm confused."

Vicki came close. "You know Carpathia is out to get believers in Christ. Can you really trust him?"

"Of course. I look up to him. He's like a god. You saw what he said, how much he loves people and cares about them. He's always here for us. He always helps us get through the hard times."

Vicki wanted to tell Marjorie what Buck Williams saw at the United Nations building. Carpathia had killed two men with one bullet, then convinced everyone except Buck that he hadn't done it. Vicki knew Marjorie wouldn't believe the story. She had to convince Marjorie another way. But how?

Judd made copies of the flyers and hurried back to Yitzhak's house. Everyone seemed excited as Mr. Stein passed out samples to the witnesses.

Mr. Stein asked everyone to write in the time of the first meeting in a blank space on the pamphlet. "We begin inviting people tomorrow. God has given us a small meeting room a few blocks from one of the government buildings."

Lionel took a stack of flyers and wrote down the information. "This is going to be great."

Nada's father, Jamal, came into the room. He touched Judd on the shoulder. "May I speak with you downstairs?"

Judd followed him to a secluded spot.

"I see now that my anger fueled my desire for revenge. God can handle Nicolae Carpathia without my help. My main concern now is Kasim," Jamal said.

"He says he's going through with his plan. He wants me to help."

"We had a disagreement. When I told him my feelings, he ran from the house. He says he's not coming back."

"What do you want me to do?"

"Stay close to him. Tell him you'll help. Then, when the time comes, we will stop him and hopefully save his life."

"I don't want to lie," Judd said.

"You're not. You *are* helping him. Do this for Lina and me. I cannot bear to lose my son again."

Vicki was still thinking when Janie spoke up. "I've got something to say."

Mark moved toward her but Vicki stopped him. "It's okay. Go ahead."

Janie leaned against the wall and nodded toward Vicki. "I met her in an awful place. It was a detention center. Wouldn't send a dog to it, but that's where we wound up. Because of her, I got out and had a chance at a new life."

Vicki said, "Janie came to live with me and my adopted dad for a while."

"What's this got to do with—"

"Just hear me out," Janie said. "I got in trouble at the high school, and they sent me away. I blamed everybody else, including Vicki, but it was my own fault. After I escaped the GC, I got lucky and found this place."

Janie rubbed her neck and looked away. "Only, I honestly don't think it was luck. I think there was somebody watching out for me. Somebody caring for me."

"So that proves there's a God?" Marjorie said.

"I've royally messed up my life. I've been into drugs. I've lied to people who were my friends." Janie faced Marjorie. "When those locusts came, these people warned me, but I wouldn't listen. When the fire and all that stinking smoke came, Vicki stuck with me."

Marjorie turned. "Vicki? You're not Vicki Byrne, are you?"

Janie said, "Sorry, Vick."

"That's okay. Yes, I'm wanted by the GC."

Marjorie sat and ran a hand through her hair.

Janie knelt before her. "What I'm saying is, these people care about you. It doesn't matter to them if you've been into drugs or if you lie or steal. They don't care if you're the most loyal follower of Carpathia there ever was. They care about you because God cares about them. They want you to know him."

"Why are you saying this?" Marjorie said.

"I've caused them no end of trouble. I used to think Enigma Babylon was the way to go, but after being here and seeing them in action, I know what they're saying's true. And you'd best believe before the next judgment hits."

Vicki stared at Janie. She couldn't believe what the girl was saying.

Janie walked back to her chair and sat. "That's all I've got to say."

The room fell silent. Vicki didn't know whether to talk with Marjorie or Janie. Mark looked stunned and sat on the floor.

Finally Marjorie said, "I know you people are sincere, and I believe you care. You could've taken my gun and shot me with it, but you didn't."

"We want you to know the truth," Vicki said. "It can change you forever." Vicki turned to Janie. "But I don't understand. If you believe what we say and that God cares about you, why don't you follow through?"

Janie smiled and looked away. "I've heard you guys say God doesn't make mistakes. Well, I think you're wrong. I'm the biggest mistake he ever made."

Vicki put a hand on the girl's shoulder. "Janie, I've prayed for you almost every day since I've known you. I've asked God to soften your heart. Don't tell me you understand and you've walked this far but you won't take the last step."

Janie put a hand to her forehead. "I don't deserve . . ."

"Don't give me that," Vicki said. "None of us deserve—"

"You don't know the stuff I've done! If you did, you'd have never taken me into your house."

"You just said it yourself—it doesn't matter. I don't care what you've done. God loves you. He wants to call you his daughter."

Janie wrapped her arms around her chest and sobbed.

Lionel sat up in bed and listened for sounds in the house. Sam and Judd slept soundly in bunks nearby. Something was wrong, but Lionel didn't know what it was.

He remembered that hot summer night when he was ten. He was sleeping at a friend's house in Chicago. A burglar had tried to crawl through a window on the other side of the room. Lionel had screamed and woken everyone up. His friend's father had caught the guy and held him until the police came.

Lionel crept into Yitzhak's living room. Nothing. He opened the door to the basement and heard snoring. He went back to bed but couldn't sleep.

"God," Lionel whispered, "maybe you woke me up for a reason. Is there something you want me to do?"

Chills went through Lionel's body. He didn't hear a voice or see a vision, but he had a strong feeling he should pray. "Okay, pray for what?"

Silence.

"God, I'll pray for anything or anyone you want me to, but tell me who."

Silence.

Lionel shook Judd awake and told him what had happened. Judd woke Sam and scampered out of the room. A few minutes later, he returned with Mr. Stein.

"God is at work with someone you know," Mr. Stein said. "Perhaps they need safety.

Perhaps they need wisdom. Many times I have felt the prayers of other believers."

"Let's start," Lionel said.

All four knelt and buried their heads in their hands. The first person Lionel prayed for was Vicki.

Vicki hadn't seen Janie cry like this since the GC took her away from Nicolae High.

"I've listened in on some of your meetings," Janie said. "I'd give anything to be part of your group, but somehow I always wind up treating you like dirt."

"God can change all that," Vicki said.

"And what if you guys take a chance on me and I let you down? I'd feel even worse after all you've done for me."

Vicki felt a tug on her shoulder. It was Marjorie. "Okay. I understand now. I want to become one of you guys. What do I do?"

Vicki looked from Janie to Marjorie and back again. "Uh, I can lead you in a prayer if you really want to do this."

"I do."

"Okay, you can say this out loud or just say it to yourself."

Marjorie clasped her hands and bowed her head. "I'm ready."

Vicki prayed. "God, I believe you're there and that you care for me. I'm sorry for the bad things I've done. Forgive me. I believe Jesus died in my place on the cross, and right now I want to receive the gift you're offering me. Change my life from the inside out. Save me from my sin and help me to follow you every day of my life. In Jesus' name, amen."

Vicki turned to Janie. "Would you like to pray too?"

Janie lifted her head and Vicki gasped. On Janie's forehead was the mark of the true believer.

Vicki hugged the girl and they both cried.

"I feel like a new person," Marjorie said.

Vicki looked at Marjorie and gasped. She had no mark.

SIX
The Hoax

VICKI tried to act cool and hugged Marjorie. Janie pointed at Vicki's forehead. "I thought you guys were making that up."

"Making what up?" Marjorie said.

Vicki turned. "Things will become clear as we go along. We'd like to get you into a class first thing in the morning."

"Great," Marjorie said, "but I really want to go back to the GC and work as a secret agent. That would help the cause, right?"

Mark stepped forward. "Sure. We could use all the information about the GC that we can get."

Janie looked puzzled. "But she doesn't have—"

Vicki held up a hand. "People who are new to the faith usually go through a few classes to learn the basics. Marjorie, why don't you room with me for the first few nights?"

"Fine."

Vicki showed Marjorie their room, then asked Mark to explain things to Janie and call an emergency meeting of the Young Trib Force.

Judd sent an e-mail to the kids at the schoolhouse and noticed an e-mail from Tsion Ben-Judah. Judd had told the rabbi all that had happened in the past few months.

Tsion wrote:

> *I am very sad to hear of the death of your friend Nada. We have all lost so many loved ones. I think about my wife and children every day, and I'm sure you will think of Nada often.*
>
> *Judd, it is important for you to grieve this loss. I find great comfort in the Psalms as the writers pour out their hearts to God. Don't pretend this didn't happen or that it's not painful. Keep a journal to write down your thoughts and feelings. I hear many people saying they need to "move on," and they miss the work God could do in them through this grief.*

Judd thought of Kasim. Instead of grieving for his sister, Kasim had immediately decided to kill Carpathia.

Judd continued reading.

> *The way you described the horsemen was exactly what I saw. Rayford Steele and others had told me about them, but I had never seen them myself. I was praying for my friend Chaim Rosenzweig when I saw them. I thought it was a dream. An army of angry horsemen filled my window. I can't imagine what it was like to see them in the middle of Jerusalem.*

Tsion spoke of the Tribulation Force's hiding place and how the summer heat was getting to them.

> *Pray for us as we work together. The bright spot in our world is baby Kenny, but he gets cranky at times and is difficult. I pray God will enable us to accomplish whatever task he gives in his power and in his timing.*

The computer beeped. A video message was coming from the schoolhouse. Judd quickly adjusted the equipment and was surprised to see Mark and Vicki.

"We have a situation here," Mark said. "We

thought you might want to have some input."

Mark explained what had happened with the satellite truck and Marjorie Amherst. Judd remembered the girl from his graduation ceremony. "If I'm right, she was the head of the drama club."

"That makes sense," Vicki said. "She's putting on an acting job."

"What do you mean?"

Vicki told Judd about Marjorie's prayer. "The good news is that Janie is now a believer. She's understood a lot more than we thought. But Marjorie doesn't have the mark."

"You think she's faking it?"

Vicki nodded. "Everyone who asks God to forgive them receives the mark. She seemed to change her attitude right after she found out my name."

"I get it," Judd said. "She's acting like a believer until she gets back to the GC. Where is she now?"

"Janie's keeping an eye on her."

"Has she seen any of the others?"

"Only a few of us," Vicki said. "We're keeping everyone else out of sight until we figure out what to do."

"Get her away from there as fast as you can. If she gets in touch with the GC, that hideout is cooked."

"I agree," Mark said.

"But what if she really changes her mind about God?" Vicki said. "It happened to Janie."

"That's your call," Judd said. "Some people are always going to be blinded to the truth. I'd say she's a huge risk."

Mark excused himself to check on Janie and Marjorie. Vicki scooted closer to the monitor. "I heard something about your friend in New Babylon dying."

Judd told Vicki about Pavel's death and how his father had helped the kids get out of New Babylon.

"What about Sam?" Vicki said. "Last I heard, you guys were looking for him."

Judd nodded. "The GC questioned him. He was released, but his father died in the last stampede of the horsemen. Sam will probably travel with us."

"I'd like to meet him. When do you think you'll come back?"

Judd told Vicki about Mr. Stein's plan to give the message of truth at the Gala.

"Sounds risky. I like it."

Judd bit his lip. "Vicki, I've got something awful to tell you." Judd explained his friendship with Nada and how it had grown. "I think you would have really liked her."

"Would have?"

Judd told Vicki what had happened the day of the final attack. When he told her how Nada had died, Vicki put a hand to her mouth. "I'm so sorry. I had no idea."

Vicki recalled a phone conversation with Mark while she was on her cross-country trip. Lionel had written briefly about Judd's girlfriend. Vicki had made fun of Nada's name. Now she felt guilty.

"I got an e-mail from Tsion that really helped," Judd said. "I'm going to look up a bunch of psalms he suggested."

Vicki moved closer to the screen. "I can't tell you how sorry I am. I wish I could be there."

Judd nodded. "When I get back, I'd like to talk. I know we've had our good and bad times. If it's okay with you, I'd like to patch things up."

"I'll look forward to talking face-to-face. And I'll be praying for you."

"Thanks. If there's anything we can do from this end about the satellite feed, let us know."

Vicki closed the connection and sat back. She felt bad for Judd's loss. She couldn't imagine what Nada's family was going through.

But there was something else to her sadness, something she couldn't explain. Was it jealousy? fear? She had to admit that the news about Judd's romance had affected her. Usually she could push her thoughts aside until she went to bed. It was then that her feelings about Judd, the past, and the next judgment came to the surface.

Vicki checked with Mark to make sure their plan for Marjorie was in place. She found Marjorie talking with Janie. Within an hour, Marjorie had begun speaking about God and Jesus and saying nothing about Nicolae Carpathia.

"It'll be such a blessing to meet the rest of the group," Marjorie said. "When can I see them?"

"I'm sure we'll work it out," Vicki said. She handed Marjorie her gun and walkie-talkie. "No need to keep these from you anymore."

Marjorie tossed her gun on the bed and looked at the GC radio. "I was going to ask God to help me figure out what's wrong with this. Does he answer prayers like that?"

"What do you want to do with it?" Janie said.

"If I can reach my superiors, I'll tell them I'm all right and I'll be back soon. Then I can report to you guys." She opened the back and gasped. "Somebody took out the solar cell."

Vicki asked Mark to come in. He brought glasses of lemonade on a tray. "Lenore thought you guys would like something to drink before bed." He handed Marjorie a glass, then let Janie and Vicki choose theirs.

Marjorie downed hers in two gulps. "Do you know anything about the solar cell?"

"Yeah, I took it out when you got here," Mark said.

"Well, go get it so I can radio headquarters. Then we'll all praise the Lord!"

Mark looked at Vicki. "Okay. I'll be right back."

"The GC is going to come looking for that truck," Marjorie said. "When I get back, I'll tell them it was destroyed."

Vicki thought about Carl. If Marjorie told the GC about the truck, Carl would be in danger. "We already took care of that. We hacked into the GC database and listed it as destroyed."

"You can do that?" Marjorie said.

Vicki yawned. "It's getting late. Maybe you should radio them in the morning."

Marjorie sat on the bed and put a hand to her head. "No, I want to call them tonight, if it's okay." She closed her eyes and opened them wide. "Is it me, or is something wrong in here?"

"Lie back," Vicki said. "You need to rest."

"Yeah, maybe a little snooze will help."

Marjorie turned her head and drifted to sleep. Janie squinted. "What's the matter with her?"

Vicki motioned Janie into the hallway and closed the door softly. "Lenore found something in the medical supplies that helps you sleep. We put it in her lemonade."

Mark ran up the stairs. "Is she out?"

Vicki nodded. "But Lenore said it won't last long."

"All right. Let's go."

Conrad joined them and helped Mark carry Marjorie to the car. Vicki got in the back to steady Marjorie during the bumpy ride to town.

"This looks good," Mark said as they approached a GC headquarters building. "I don't want to get too close and have them spot us with a surveillance camera."

Conrad stopped, and the three carefully placed Marjorie on the ground. Mark hooked up the solar cell to the walkie-talkie and handed it to Vicki. "You've always wanted to be a Morale Monitor, right?"

Vicki smiled and clicked the radio. "Headquarters, this is Morale Monitor Marjorie Amherst. I'm in trouble. Need help. I'm just a couple of blocks from headquarters on the side of the road."

Vicki slurred her speech and said, "I'm passing out. Help me. Please."

Vicki fastened the radio to the holder on Marjorie's shoulder and jumped in the car. Conrad drove into a nearby alley. Moments later a GC patrol car pulled up to the curb and two uniformed officers got out.

"She's okay," Mark said. "Let's go."

"You think the GC will believe her story?" Vicki said.

"They will when she tells them about the satellite truck," Mark said.

Vicki slept late the next morning. Janie was waiting for her when she came into the kitchen. A Bible and a notebook were open on the table. "I'm ready to learn. I promise I'll listen and take notes this time."

Judd helped Mr. Stein and the others prepare for their first meeting. Everyone was excited at the response from people on the street. Some had thrown the pamphlets down, but others eagerly read the information. Many had said they would attend.

Judd found a note on his bed the afternoon of the first meeting. "Meet me at 5:00 P.M. Tell no one." Underneath was an address. Judd stuffed the paper in his pocket and told Lionel he was going out.

"What about the meeting?"

"I'll be back."

The Global Community had tried to make things seem normal, but how could anything be normal with a third of the world's population dead? Bodies had been removed from the streets, but there was still the smell of charred buildings in the air.

He found the address and buzzed the correct apartment. The door to the entrance clicked, and Judd walked inside and up two flights of stairs. A single bare bulb lighted the hallway. Judd had to squint to read the apartment numbers.

Kasim opened the door and let Judd inside. There was a table and a couple of chairs but not much more. The refrigerator was old and smelled funny. "Love what you've done with the place."

Kasim motioned Judd to the window and opened a curtain. "I'm not here to decorate. I'm here for the view. Look."

The window looked out on a huge plaza. There were shops to the right and left, then an open area. "What is it?"

"I broke into the main GC computer in

New Babylon. "That's where they'll build the stage. This window will give me a clear shot."

Judd closed his eyes. "You mean at Carpathia?"

Kasim nodded and pulled out his handgun. "But I have a problem. I need to find some kind of rifle with a scope. This won't reach that far with any accuracy."

"Why are you telling me this?"

"You have to help me find one. The people I bought this from are upset. You can travel freely. I can't."

"No thanks."

Kasim opened a nearby Bible to Revelation 13. "It says in here that one of the heads of the beast will be fatally wounded. I think that's Nicolae, and I'm going to be the one to wound him."

SEVEN

Answered Prayer

VICKI and the others worried that Marjorie's return to the GC would trigger a search for the satellite truck, so the kids pulled the truck into the woods below the schoolhouse. Conrad showed them an old logging road that ran by the river, and the kids parked the truck near it. Charlie and Shelly scoured the surrounding woods for branches and limbs to cover the truck. When they were finished, it was completely hidden.

"The best chance they have of spotting it is from the air," Mark said.

"You can't see it from above," Conrad said. "The satellite dish is out in the open, but it's pretty small."

Over the next few days the kids monitored GC satellite transmissions. The head of the Global Community Department of Education, Dr. Neal Damosa, outlined his future plans at a press conference. Before the transmission, Damosa talked with an aide as they clipped on a microphone. A huge mural of New Babylon was placed behind him.

"Here are the notes you requested, sir," the aide said.

Someone tipped the painting and it nearly fell on Damosa. The man cursed and screamed at the work crew. "That happens again and I'll have you all fired."

Conrad looked at Vicki. "I wonder if that's how Carpathia acts off the air?"

"He's probably worse," Vicki said.

Damosa scanned the notes. "I asked for numbers of dead in the age range—"

The aide quickly turned the pages and said, "Page three, sir."

Damosa studied the numbers. "We have lost a third of those eligible for attendance. But it has just become easier to keep track of all our students. That is our goal, you know. We want to track every person alive. Have the security measures been stepped up?"

"Yes, sir. In addition to the Morale Monitors, we will have Peacekeeping presence as well."

"Good. The Morale Monitors can ferret out our enemies, but they are helpless when the attacks occur."

"The Monitors now wear stun guns. If they suspect a Judah-ite in attendance, they have been instructed to stun the individual and ask questions later."

Damosa smiled. "I doubt there will be many Judah-ites at our next lessons."

"We'll be ready if they come."

Mark wrote something on a scrap of paper. "I want everybody to know about the stun guns. I'll put it on the Web site pronto."

The aide fussed with Damosa's collar as someone shouted cues. Reporters took their places in front of the podium. Finally, Damosa went on the air. When the cameras were on, his scowl turned to a warm smile.

"This guy is almost as good as Carpathia," Conrad said.

"Before I take questions, I have a brief statement," Damosa said. "I come to you with a heavy heart, knowing that many who were with us at our first meeting are no longer alive. Now more than ever, we need those of the younger generation to understand the importance of their contribution. In spite of the danger of possible attack, we will send a message to our enemies that we will not be intimidated by their terrorist tactics."

Vicki shook her head. "I don't know how

they can blame believers for this and get away with it."

Damosa continued. "This is a time of great fear. It would be easy to panic or simply stay in the safety of your homes. By attending the satellite schools, we show that we will not cower. Just as Potentate Carpathia has led us in the pathway of peace, so our young people will strive toward that same goal.

"Therefore, I urge everyone up to and including the age of twenty to attend our next session. We have many surprises in store, and your safety is our utmost priority."

Vicki noticed Charlie in the back of the truck drawing something. When she asked to see it, Charlie turned the page around. It was a replica of the picture behind Damosa.

"That's pretty good," Shelly said.

Vicki took the paper. "It's better than pretty good. It's perfect. Where did you learn to do this?"

"I've been able to draw since I was little. I'm better at buildings than people."

Vicki handed the drawing back to Charlie. "Do you think you could do that on a big sheet of paper? or maybe on a wall?"

"Sure. Why?"

"If we're going to break into a GC telecast, I want them to think it's something coming from New Babylon."

Vicki heard a strange noise. "Is that coming from the satellite feed?"

Mark turned down the volume, but the sound was still there.

Conrad opened the door. The droning grew louder. "It's a plane or maybe a chopper."

"Quick! Hide the dish!" Mark said.

Conrad leaped from the truck and threw a sheet over the satellite dish. When he was safely inside, Vicki shut the door.

"That's definitely a chopper," Conrad said. "Probably GC."

The kids listened as the helicopter drew close. Vicki's heart beat faster and faster. What would the kids do if the GC spotted their hideout?

Judd walked to the meeting in a daze. Now that Kasim had his own apartment, he would be harder to stop. It wasn't that Judd cared for Carpathia. The man was the enemy of their souls. Judd didn't want Kasim to get hurt or bring the GC down on their group.

When Judd entered the small meeting room, he saw his friends surrounded by forty to fifty people. Some were young, others old. A few were Orthodox Jews and stood to the side. People sat in metal folding chairs arranged in a semicircle.

Mr. Stein got everyone's attention. "We have prayed for you," he began. "As we passed out the flyers, we asked God to draw those open to truth. We praise him for your presence tonight."

A few of the Orthodox Jews headed for the door. Mr. Stein took a step forward. "Please, my friends, don't go until you have heard our message."

One man turned. "We are not your friend and we do not serve the same God as you."

Holding out his hands, Mr. Stein approached the man. "We agree about many things. There is one God. Nicolae Carpathia is not who he claims to be. He is not our ruler and king."

The man nodded. "You are right. We have watched Carpathia closely and do not believe he is truly a man of peace."

"God above has given you this wisdom. But many will turn from the true and living God to serve this man of sin."

"We may agree about this, but we cannot follow your teaching about the one you call the Christ."

Mr. Stein smiled. "I was once like you. I did not accept the claims of Jesus as the Messiah. When my daughter told me she had turned from my faith, I counted her as dead. I turned my back on her."

"As well you should," the man said. Others agreed.

Mr. Stein asked for his Bible. Lionel brought it to him. "I admire your faith and your zeal. But as the Bible predicts, our society will become more and more sinful. Soon, even to this holy city, there will be such great evil and wickedness. And one day in the future, the temple you now worship God in shall be defiled by the Antichrist."

"How could you know such things?" the man said. "Are you a prophet?"

"I am a humble follower of the King of kings and Lord of lords. He has given me and others the ability to speak in different languages so that everyone may hear the truth."

The group grumbled and urged the man to leave. Mr. Stein pleaded, but one by one the Orthodox Jews filed out of the room. Mr. Stein bowed his head. He returned to the front of the room, weeping.

Vicki and the others listened to the chopper pass. Mark peeked out the back window. "It's GC all right, but I don't think they slowed down as they went over the schoolhouse."

"That was way too close," Vicki said. "We have to be ready to get out of here fast."

"Already got that covered," Conrad said. He took a sheet of paper from Charlie and marked the escape route. Vicki couldn't believe the detail of the plan.

"This is only if the GC find us, right?" Charlie said.

Conrad nodded. "I'd like to remove some equipment from the truck and set it up downstairs. Then we can pull the truck a little farther onto the logging road."

Vicki nodded. "Let's get the equipment out of here. Charlie, you start on the painting. Choose a room downstairs and make one of the walls as much like the picture we saw on TV as you can."

"Got it," Charlie said.

The kids stopped when they heard the *thwock thwock thwock* of the chopper again.

Judd prayed as Mr. Stein composed himself and stood before the group. People turned to each other and talked, many in different languages.

"We want to tell you the best news you could ever hear. We want to tell you how you can have true peace with God and live with him forever."

The people stopped talking as Mr. Stein read or recited several Bible verses. Something shuffled outside in the shadows, but Judd couldn't make out what or who it was.

Suddenly the door burst open and three Global Community Peacekeepers charged in with rifles drawn. "Hands up! Everyone!"

Everyone obeyed except Mr. Stein. He stepped toward the men. "What is this about? We have no quarrel with you."

"Hands in the air!" the Peacekeeper shouted. "This is an unlawful assembly. You will all be arrested and questioned."

Several in the audience started crying. Lionel got Judd's attention and nodded toward a back door. Judd shook his head. He didn't want to risk getting shot by running.

Mr. Stein knelt. "Our Father, we have been faithful to the task you have given. If you desire us to speak about you to those in authority, we will gladly do so. But we ask your divine protection on these who have not yet been able to respond—"

The lead Peacekeeper kicked Mr. Stein in the side. "On your feet, old man!"

Mr. Stein slumped to the ground as Judd rushed to help him. A woman nearby leaned down and whispered, "If we believe what you are saying, what are we to do?"

Mr. Stein closed his eyes. "Lord, give us enough time to show these people how to respond to you."

Someone gasped and another man cried out. Judd looked up as all three Peacekeepers fell backward. Two darted outside and ran away. The third landed on the floor, his gun clattering against a metal chair. The man pulled his knees to his chest and shook with fear. "Please, don't hurt me!"

Judd picked up the gun and walked to the man. "I'm not going to hurt you."

"Not you." The man's eyes were as big as saucers as he pointed toward Mr. Stein. "Them."

Judd turned. The room looked the same as it had all night. "Who are you talking about?"

"Those two beside the guy with the beard."

Judd looked again. The Peacekeeper was clearly pointing toward Mr. Stein, but there was no one beside him.

"What do they look like?" Judd said.

"Big. Shiny. It hurts to look at them. And they have weapons! Please, tell them not to hurt me."

"It's okay," Judd said, trying to figure out what the man had seen. "Leave now and you won't be hurt."

The Peacekeeper stood and ran out the door.

Judd turned to Mr. Stein. "What was that all about?"

Mr. Stein smiled. "God has protected us again. We asked for his help and he has given it."

EIGHT

The Ambassador

WHEN the helicopter was gone, Vicki and the others helped Conrad remove equipment from the satellite truck. Though some of the gear was permanently attached, Conrad took enough inside for the kids to watch the satellite school transmissions and make their own recording.

Mark called Carl to find out how they could uplink Vicki's video. Since Janie was the newest believer, Vicki asked her to help craft an explanation of the truth.

"Carl says you'll probably have about five minutes, tops, before the GC figure out how to jam the signal," Mark said. "We'll record ten to fifteen minutes just in case, but make sure you get the important stuff up front."

"How do we get the video to Carl?"

"Still working on it," Mark said. "Hopefully we can align the dish and let Carl take care of the rest."

Vicki scribbled notes of things she wanted to say. Janie and Melinda told her what had helped most in changing their minds about God. Vicki had written several pages when Conrad asked them to come into the new control room.

The basement had been transformed into a television studio. Conrad had the camera set up near the wall Charlie was painting. A huge monitor sat in the corner.

"It'll take some time to figure out how to link up with Carl," Conrad said, "but we can record as soon as you guys are ready."

Charlie had draped a sheet over two ladders to keep his painting private. Vicki asked if she could come in, but Charlie said he wanted to wait until he was finished.

"How much longer?"

"I'll work through the night. Should be ready by tomorrow afternoon."

Vicki typed her notes into the computer so she could read them from the monitor. She wanted everything about the recording to be perfect. "Can we put any kinds of graphics or messages across the bottom?"

Conrad smiled. "Just tell me what you want me to put on the screen."

After the Peacekeepers had run from the room, many people stood to leave. Mr. Stein tried to stop them.

"We don't want them to come back and shoot us!" one man said.

"Stay and hear the message!" Mr. Stein said.

"If we leave, will you kill us?" another asked.

"Of course not."

Mr. Stein talked about Jesus to the few who remained. When he was through, several prayed. One man who had just prayed approached Judd. He was older with a square jaw and piercing eyes. He had a powerful handshake and towered over Judd. "You are American. Do you have a place to stay?"

"Yes, but there are others passing through who might need somewhere to sleep."

The man handed Judd a card. "I have many rooms in my house. One as big as this. Tell your friends. I will be back tomorrow night with my neighbors."

When they returned to Yitzhak's house, Judd asked Mr. Stein why the Peacekeepers had run.

"This also happened during my trip to Africa. The Bible shows many examples of angels helping people. I fear tonight we were in very serious trouble, but the Almighty protected us."

Lionel nodded. "If that's true, maybe we shouldn't go back to the same place two nights in a row. The GC could be waiting for us."

Mr. Stein scratched his beard. "You're right. But where do we go? And how do we let people know we've moved the meeting?"

Judd pulled out the man's card from earlier that night. "This man said he has a lot of room at his house."

Yitzhak squinted as he read the man's name.

"What is it?" Lionel said.

"This man is one of Israel's leading military planners. They call him the General. He lives near Chaim Rosenzweig's estate."

One of the witnesses said, "Who is Chaim Rosenzweig?"

Sam stood. "Only one of the most famous men in all of Israel. He discovered a formula that makes the desert bloom like a garden."

Judd said, "Some in the Tribulation Force are talking to him about God."

Mr. Stein took the paper. "General Solomon Zimmerman. We must go and see this man."

Vicki gasped when she saw the detail of Charlie's work. The painting had intricate details of the New Babylon skyline. The kids and Lenore clapped when they saw it. Little Tolan giggled and laughed as Charlie held him in his arms.

"Almost looks like you could walk right into it," Darrion said.

Vicki winked at Conrad. "Let's get started."

Since Mark had the deepest voice, Vicki had him read a brief introduction. Mark tried to sound like a GC announcer, but laughed when Conrad made a face. After a few tries he got through the introduction, and Conrad played it back.

"In cooperation with the Global Community Department of Education, we proudly present the new ambassador to the next generation, Connie Goodwill."

Conrad found an instrumental fanfare and mixed it under Mark's voice. The kids were amazed. "This is where we fade up on Vicki—"

"You mean, Connie," Shelly said.

"Right," Conrad said. "We'll start with Connie sitting in front of Charlie's painting."

Lenore slipped out and returned with something on a hanger. "Charlie's not the only one with talent. Z sent some material in his last supply shipment, and I tried to match that Damosa character's suit. Here's what I came up with."

Lenore unveiled a new outfit for Vicki that looked almost exactly like Dr. Damosa's suit. On the shoulder was the insignia of the Global Community.

"Where did you get the insignia?" Vicki said.

Lenore smiled. "Just get dressed and record your message, Ambassador."

Judd shook his head as he walked into the courtyard of Solomon Zimmerman's home. When he had seen the man the night before, the General looked like any other person off the street. Now, standing in the midst of what seemed like a tropical garden, Judd saw that he was a man of great wealth and stature.

A man in uniform led Judd and the others inside. They waited in a foyer until General Zimmerman met them and showed them into his massive library. While Mr. Stein talked about using the house for the next meeting, Judd studied the volumes that lined the man's bookshelves. There were biographies of great military leaders, works of fiction about warfare, volumes of reference material, and even different translations of the Bible.

The General said he would be delighted to have them meet in his home. Before they left, Mr. Stein asked how the General had heard of their meeting.

"One of my aides found a flyer on the street. I have seen much death and bloodshed in my career, but these last few years have been extraordinary. I was curious to hear your explanation last night, and in the process, I discovered the truth."

"Weren't you in command when the nuclear attack against Israel began?" Yitzhak said.

General Zimmerman closed his eyes and nodded. "I remember it like it was yesterday. I suppose that's when I first began to think there might be a God." The General looked at Judd. "I saw you looking at my books. Are you surprised I have copies of the Bible?"

Judd nodded. "If you didn't believe in God, why would you have them?"

"I studied the Bible because to me it was a book of warfare. In my military history classes I learned, and later taught, about the many battles described in what you call the Old Testament. There is great wisdom in the way Gideon divided his men, the way King David attacked the Philistines, and of course,

God's soldier Joshua, and the way he took Jericho. In all the time I studied those battles, I never considered them of any spiritual importance. They were simply stories. Now that I know the truth, they are much more than stories."

"What happened when the Russians attacked?" Lionel said. "We studied this in school, but I'd like to hear your version."

General Zimmerman smiled. "I suppose we have my neighbor to blame." He pointed out the window. "If Dr. Rosenzweig had not created the formula that literally changed the landscape of our country, perhaps we would not have been attacked."

"The Russians wanted the formula?" Lionel said.

"Russia's economy had been devastated. All they had was military might. When Israel prospered, they were determined to occupy the Holy Land. We had an inkling something bad was coming, but we had no idea it would be an all-out attack."

"Didn't it come in the middle of the night?" Judd said.

General Zimmerman nodded. "I was awakened and told missiles were heading toward our largest cities. Fighter-bombers with nuclear weapons flew overhead as I reached our defense headquarters. We had no time to ask for help. We were outnumbered one hundred to one. But we had to act.

"We launched surface-to-air missiles toward the enemy, and the first ones hit their targets. But the number of missiles attacking us was overwhelming. Our radar screens were filled with targets we could not possibly destroy.

"Then the explosions began. Planes slammed to earth. We knew the end was near. But we discovered the planes were falling from the sky without us shooting them down. The Russians' nuclear weapons exploded high above the earth. The sky was on fire and night turned to the brightest daylight. You cannot imagine the heat."

General Zimmerman ran a hand through his hair. "I went outside the bunker. I figured we were all dead anyway. Then came the hail, which turned to freezing rain. After a few minutes, the fire in the sky went out and darkness settled in, along with deathly silence. The entire Russian air attack was consumed in fire that night."

"What did you think happened?" Lionel said.

"Some believed it was a meteor shower, but how could such a thing happen and not harm one living soul on the ground? How could so many planes crash and burn without killing anyone except the pilots? I have asked that question many times, but I have not come up with a believable answer until now. Now I know that God protected Israel like he protected us last night."

The General explained what had happened since the rise of the Global Community. Zimmerman said he had never fully trusted Nicolae Carpathia, and now that he knew the truth about God, he cringed at what would happen during the Gala.

"We have other plans while that celebration occurs," Mr. Stein said.

"Tell me," General Zimmerman said. "I want to help tell others the truth."

It took Vicki a number of takes to get through her message. She felt nervous with others watching her and asked them to leave the room.

"Hundreds of thousands are going to see this," Conrad said.

"I know it's silly, but I'd feel better if it was just you and me in here."

When she finished, Conrad began editing. "Shouldn't take me more than a couple days to have the final product."

"How did you learn how to do this?"

"My brother had a pretty sophisticated computer with a lot of video and editing software. He used to let me play around on it."

Conrad's voice trailed off. It had been a while since Vicki had asked about Taylor Graham. She said, "I bet you miss him."

Conrad nodded. "When we're in the middle of a project like this, I stay focused. But at other times, like when we were driving cross-country, I think about him a lot. I wish I'd had more time to talk with him."

Vicki put a hand on Conrad's shoulder. "Maybe what you're doing here will help a lot of kids know the truth."

For the next few days the kids watched the news and the countdown to the return of the satellite schools. Conrad finished Vicki's recording and played it for the entire Young Trib Force. Charlie beamed when he saw his painting. Everyone was impressed with Vicki and for fun called her "the Ambassador."

Finally the day arrived when Dr. Neal Damosa appeared before cheering crowds around the world. The kids watched closely and took notes on the latest teaching from the Global Community.

Mark tapped Vicki on the shoulder and asked her to come upstairs. His face was grim.

"The helicopter's not back, is it?" Vicki said.

Mark shook his head. "When we brought the stuff in from the truck we must have damaged the satellite. We can't get the signal to Carl."

"What does that mean?"

"Unless we come up with another plan, no one will see your recording but us."

NINE

On the Air

OVER the next few weeks, Judd and the others held meetings nightly at General Zimmerman's home. Some nights there were only ten or fifteen people, but as time went on and more heard about Mr. Stein's teaching, General Zimmerman's house began to look like a convention center. People hungry for the truth returned with neighbors and friends. Mr. Stein was elated.

Judd spent little time at Yitzhak's house and hoped Kasim would forget his assassination plan. But a conversation with Jamal changed that.

"Kasim came here late last night looking for you," Jamal said.

"Did you tell him where we're meeting?"

"I mentioned the General's house, and his eyes lit up for some reason. I wouldn't be surprised if he shows up for a meeting there."

That night Mr. Stein asked Judd to tell his story. As the meeting began, Kasim walked in. He smiled at Judd.

"You thought you could avoid me, Judd? Aren't you going to help me with the plan?"

"No," Judd said. "I'm sorry. And I think you should—"

Kasim interrupted. "But you led me here, right? You're helping me without even knowing it."

"What are you talking about?"

"General Zimmerman is known for his collection of military weapons. Where does he keep them?"

General Zimmerman had given Judd and the others a tour of his home and had shown them guns dating back to the American Civil War. There were swords and shields from the Roman Empire. And, as Kasim believed, the collection upstairs also contained some of the most recent weaponry.

"Come to the front and tell your story," Mr. Stein said. People turned and looked at Judd.

"Don't do this," Judd whispered to Kasim.

Judd was almost finished with his story when Kasim walked down the steps with something under his arm. He caught Judd's attention and held out a rifle. Seconds later Kasim was out the door and gone.

Vicki wished she could help Mark and Conrad with the satellite feed, but the maze of wires and electronic equipment overwhelmed her. The kids worked frantically to link up, but nothing worked. The next satellite school transmission was hours away, and the Gala was fast approaching.

"Can't we mail the recording to Carl?" Vicki said.

"The GC inspects all the packages," Mark said. "We should have taken it to him."

Conrad talked with Carl in Florida and tried different switches. "Let me put you on the speaker."

"Isn't this dangerous for you, Carl?" Vicki said.

"I'm off duty in a truck parked next to our main studio," Carl said. "I'm okay as long as they don't catch me."

"What do we do now?" Conrad said.

"Try it again. If we can get this to work, I'll record here and then figure out how to put it on the main feed to the stadiums."

Tolan crawled into the room and bumped against the door. He wailed. Conrad yelled, "Get that kid out of here!"

Vicki picked Tolan up and comforted him.

Lenore came and took him upstairs. Vicki knew the pressure of the uplink and the summer heat had everyone frazzled.

The satellite schools attracted record crowds of kids around the world. More were attending and seemed to buy what was being taught by the speakers. It was the perfect time to break in with their message, but Vicki worried that their plan was going to fail.

The satellite school was popular because of the top-notch celebrities and entertainment. Each broadcast featured a film star, a sports celebrity, or a musical artist who would praise the work of the Global Community. On the Friday before the GC Gala, the kids were surprised to see a stage in the shape of a dove.

"What are they going to do with that?" Shelly said.

Vicki shook her head. "Whatever it is, it's part of the GC's brainwashing."

Lionel convinced Judd and the others to let him go to Teddy Kollek Stadium to observe the latest satellite presentation. Mr. Stein reluctantly agreed when Lionel promised he would stay outside and watch on the huge monitors. Lionel grabbed a stack of flyers and headed out the door.

The sun was setting orange and yellow as Lionel neared the stadium. Someone tapped him on the shoulder. It was Sam.

"You can't be here," Lionel said. "The GC could recognize—"

"Stop. We're both taking a chance."

Lionel pointed to a small, box-shaped shack outside Teddy Kollek Stadium. Around the structure were free handouts. A sign above said "Read the Latest from Tsion Ben-Judah!"

"They must think we're stupid," Lionel said.

A few kids in black clothes passed the shack and jeered. One grabbed a few pamphlets and tore them up. Another tried to set fire to the canopy that hung over the racks. Soon a crowd had gathered and kids chanted, "Death to Ben-Judah! Death to Ben-Judah!"

Sam frowned. "Looks like the GC's training is working."

A husky boy ran at the structure and hit it full force, like a linebacker tackling a running back. Boards cracked and pamphlets flew into the air. A window opened and two uniformed Peacekeepers with video equipment shooed the kids away.

While the Peacekeepers tried to repair the damage, Lionel spotted a GC motorcade. They drove straight into the stadium and onto the field near the dove-shaped stage.

The cars were greeted with a deafening roar. First out of a long, black limo was the head of GC education, Dr. Neal Damosa. He ran onstage like a rock star.

Sam tapped Lionel on the shoulder and pointed behind them, where a huge transport plane approached. Lionel shrugged and moved closer to the monitor.

"Fellow citizens of the Global Community, I welcome you in the name of peace!"

The stadium roared again as people inside and outside came to their feet. Lionel noticed there was a delay between what happened inside the stadium and what he was seeing on the monitor.

The plane passed directly over the stadium and banked left. Several objects fell out a side door. Lionel counted ten specks falling toward earth.

Damosa quieted the crowd and took control. "We come in peace, in a place of peace—Jerusalem. This city and its people were made a promise by Potentate Carpathia more than three years ago, a promise that has been kept. And so we gather on this stage and stand on this symbol of unity and peace, where in a few short days there will be a celebration like no other in the history of the world."

Again the crowd cheered. Damosa invited young people from every continent to join them in Jerusalem. He pointed to the sky. "Watch and see the precision of the Global Community, as members of the Peacekeeping Paratroopers descend to this very stage!"

The parachutes opened, and the ten slowly fell to earth. An announcer read the names of each Peacekeeper, one from each of Nicolae Carpathia's ten regions. Smoke trailed from the paratroopers as one by one they landed on different points of the dove. At each landing, the crowd screamed and yelled. When only one paratrooper was left, Damosa ran to a small platform in the center of the stage.

"The final member of the team will attempt to land right where I'm standing, carrying a flag with the insignia of the Global Community."

"He's going to try and land on that little square?" Sam said.

Lionel nodded. "These people are good."

The announcer called the name of the last jumper, a female from the United Carpathian States. The crowd hushed as she floated over the stadium, spinning in a circle. When she fell quickly, the crowd gasped and Lionel thought she was out of control. Suddenly, she pushed the toggles she held and landed perfectly on the small *X* in the middle of the platform.

The crowd went wild. A searchlight flashed in the sky, and thousands of doves flew through the light. Drums beat while cameras followed the flight of the birds. A screaming electric guitar pierced the air, and the cameras focused on the stage, which was completely enveloped by fog.

"It's that smoke and fire again!" someone next to Lionel said.

The crowd panicked. Dr. Damosa walked forward calmly. "We told you to expect something special, and here they are, live, The Four Horsemen!"

Lionel shook his head as the most popular band in the world launched into their wild and frenzied music. They had risen to fame a few months earlier with their song "Hoofbeats." They bashed Tsion Ben-Judah, Christianity, Jesus, and anything to do with the underground church. Lionel wasn't surprised that the Global Community embraced the group, but to link them with the satellite schools was a stroke of genius on their part.

Kids clapped, screamed, and sang along with lead singer Z-Van. He wore wraparound sunglasses and a skintight outfit that made Lionel wonder how he could possibly dance around the edge of the stage without falling off. GC security allowed kids to stream onto the infield and surround the huge dove.

Z-Van screamed his lyrics and the audience screamed back. When the first song was over, he stood on the edge of the dove, spread his arms wide, and fell backward into the crowd. The music rose, and the singer belted out more hateful lyrics as he rode the crowd like a surfboard.

Vicki peeked into the makeshift control room. Carl was on the phone going over their connections from the room to the satellite truck again with Conrad. "What happens when you try the auto-alignment?"

"It still reads *Error,*" Conrad said. "I've tried it a million times."

"Shut the whole system down. We'll start over," Carl said.

Mark flipped switches, and the monitors went dead. The kids in the other room, still watching the Four Horsemen on TV, asked what had happened. Vicki explained.

"I used to really like these guys," Janie said. "Now I think they're sick. I wish they knew the truth."

Vicki asked everyone to pray. One by one, the kids asked God to do something miraculous.

Conrad motioned Vicki inside the control

room. "I'm sorry about yelling at Tolan. I'm just—"

"It's okay," Vicki said. "You can give Lenore some free baby-sitting when this is over."

Conrad smiled. "It's a deal."

"Powering up!" Mark said as he flipped switches throughout the room. A few moments later the band was back on the monitors. Z-Van was now wearing a horse costume. As he sang, flames shot into the air.

Shelly put a hand on Vicki's shoulder. "Their music is bad, but you have to admit they're kind of cute."

Vicki shook her head. "All of their songs are just twisted lyrics from Dr. Ben-Judah's e-mail messages. I can't get past that."

"Okay, I have a green light on the controller," Conrad said. "I think the auto-alignment's working."

Mark turned on the camera and pointed it toward Charlie's painting. "Carl, if this is working right you should be—"

"I'm getting something from New Babylon."

Mark walked in front of the camera and waved. "How about now?"

"Wow!" Carl said. "I thought that was real. Great job on the painting."

"So you have us?" Conrad said.

"Picture's perfect. Let me get ready to record." Carl tapped at his keyboard and his computer blipped. "Okay. Go ahead and upload the drop-in."

Conrad searched the hard drive and inserted a different disk in the computer.

"What's wrong?" Vicki said.

"It's not here. When we powered down, we must have lost it."

The noise from the concert rose as The Four Horsemen ended a song. Z-Van threw the microphone into the air and caught it behind his back. "This will be our last tune before we take a break. Then Dr. Damosa has a few words. Put your hands together and help us out on this one!" The crowd went wild as drums beat and fireworks shot from all sides of the stage.

Vicki shook her head. "This would be the perfect time to play the message."

"You're right," Carl said, "and after the band finishes, you'll be on."

"What do you mean?" Vicki said. "We can't find the recording."

"Forget the recording. We're going live!"

TEN
Live!

VICKI stared at the phone, then looked at Mark and Conrad. "Is he serious?"

Mark nodded. "Can you get back into your GC getup? This song won't last long."

"But how—"

"I'll put your script on the monitor," Conrad said. "You'll be even better live than on the recording."

Janie ran upstairs. "I'll get the outfit for you."

Conrad pulled up the text of Vicki's message as Mark checked in with Carl. "How are you going to jam this onto the main GC signal?"

"I checked the wiring a few days ago and rigged the truck just for this. The guys inside think they have control, but I routed the main signal through here."

"What if they figure it out?"

"I've got a tiny camera in the GC control

room," Carl said. "I'll monitor them and switch back to the main feed if they get close."

"Are you sure you'll be safe?"

"They don't know I'm here. If Vicki plays it cool and takes direction, we'll be fine. Remember, we'll only have four or five minutes."

Janie returned with the clothes and Vicki changed in the downstairs bathroom. When she came out, the band finished their song and the crowd went wild. The Four Horsemen waved and hurried offstage.

"Get in position!" Conrad said.

Mark picked up the phone. "I'll relay any directions. We don't want the GC hearing Carl's voice in the background."

Vicki grabbed Janie's arm. "Get the others and pray."

The sound was deafening as Lionel stood outside the arena. Thousands cheered and fireworks exploded overhead. Cameras panned the stadium, showing kids screaming and waving cigarette lighters in the dark.

Finally the audience settled, and the camera focused on Dr. Damosa. Before he could speak, the picture switched to a scene in New Babylon. A girl in a suit walked in front of the camera.

"Pretty cool concert, brought to you by your friends at the Global Community Department of Education. We'll get back to The Four Horsemen and Dr. Neal Damosa in just a moment, but first an information time-out."

"I don't believe it!" Lionel said.

"What's wrong?" Sam said.

"That's a friend of mine. Vicki. This is going to really be cool."

Vicki felt the heat of the overhead light as she continued. What she had written for the recorded version didn't seem appropriate now, so Vicki improvised.

"My name is Vicki B. I'm the new ambassador to youth for the Global Community. On behalf of Dr. Damosa, the Peacekeepers, Morale Monitors, and our potentate, Nicolae Carpathia, I want to thank you all for making this satellite school program a huge success."

Carl Meninger's hands trembled inside the satellite truck in Florida. As he listened to Vicki, he studied the control room inside the GC Communications Compound. When Carl had first switched to Vicki, several people jumped. The engineer held his hands over the console and said, "I didn't do that. What's going on?"

Carl heard them through a tiny speaker near his monitor. Just as Carl was about to switch back to the regular feed, someone said, "Oh, this must be one of those drop-in segments."

"Yeah," another said. "They're probably feeding this from Israel."

"I can see why they picked this girl. She's cute."

Vicki wanted to be calm and just read the script, but something told her to wing it. Be creative. She knew she had to connect with viewers. If they sensed she was nervous, they would tune out.

Vicki ran a hand through her hair and said, "You know, it's a good idea to analyze the lyrics of songs. I used to listen to whatever was on the radio, and I told myself the words didn't really matter. But as a peace-loving follower of Nicolae Carpathia, you need to understand what people are saying.

"A good place to start tonight is Z-Van's lyrics. The latest Four Horsemen recording is 'Praying to Air.' I don't know all the words, but in the chorus Z-Van sings, 'You're praying to air, you're talking to sky, your mind's full of mush, 'cause you're willing to die . . . for a book.'

"What Z-Van is talking about there, of course, are the followers of Rabbi Tsion Ben-Judah. Some call them Judah-ites. Others say they're followers of Jesus. Whatever you want to call them, you have to admit there's a lot of them out there.

"The book Z-Van refers to is the Bible. As a matter of fact, I have one right here."

Lionel listened closely as Vicki read different verses. Some in the stadium booed when she pulled out the Bible, but most who were outside watched and listened with their arms folded. They seemed a little skeptical, but Vicki had their interest.

"I wonder how they're pulling this off," Sam said.

"I don't know, but this is the best thing I've seen in a long time."

Carl watched Vicki and smiled. He checked the clock. Three minutes into the broadcast.

A phone rang in the GC control room.

Carl turned Vicki down as he watched the engineer sit up straight in his chair. "No, sir. We thought it was coming from you." A long pause. "Yes, sir. Right on it, sir."

The engineer slammed the phone down. "The feed's not coming from them."

"Then where—"

"I don't know. Just figure out a way to cut this girl off. Now!"

Carl grabbed the phone. "I'm going to have to cut Vicki off. Give her thirty seconds."

Vicki watched Mark type "30 seconds" on the screen. Vicki nodded.

"So, while many people call the followers of Ben-Judah crazy, weirdos, and even dangerous, we all have to admit that what this rabbi has been saying has come true.

"Think about that. Potentate Carpathia says we should be tolerant of other beliefs and religions. Maybe it would be helpful to talk more about what these Judah-ites think in our next segment.

"I'm Vicki B. Let's get back to the fun."

The feed switched to Teddy Kollek Stadium. The audience sat in silence until a frazzled Dr. Damosa came on the screen.

"Perfect, Vicki," Mark said. "Carl says congratulations. Your timing's flawless."

"Yeah, but why did you use your real name?" Conrad said.

Vicki shrugged. "It just kind of happened. I think it sounds better than Connie Goodwill. When can I go on again?"

"Stand by," Mark said.

Carl watched the GC control room settle. The engineer had hit every switch and turned every knob possible. Just as Vicki had finished, they hit a power switch and Carl switched back to Jerusalem.

"Leave that off," the engineer yelled. "It must have something to do with it."

Carl asked to be put on the schoolhouse speakerphone. He praised Vicki for her poise. "You're a natural at this. Ought to have your own show."

"But I didn't get to what I really wanted to say."

"You will," Carl said. "When you come back on, you'll have the whole place in the palm of your hand. Damosa's supposed to speak for about twenty minutes and then bring the band back. Listen to what he says, and we'll cut to you before he introduces the band."

"I'll be ready," Vicki said.

Lionel was stunned at what the kids back home had accomplished. How they had tapped into the international satellite feed, he couldn't tell. But they had done it.

Dr. Damosa cleared his throat and gave a nervous smile. "Well, that was an interesting perspective. I'm not sure who Vicki B. is, but we'll have to have a talk with her."

Lionel whispered to Sam, "Sounds like the GC have no idea what's up."

Carl watched the control room on his monitor and listened closely for anyone moving outside his own satellite truck. He wanted to give Vicki one more chance on the air.

A phone rang in the control room. "We didn't put her on!" the engineer yelled. When he hung up, he said, "Here's the scoop. Headquarters says a Morale Monitor in Illinois recognized this Vicki B. character. She's one of those Ben-Judah followers."

"How could she hack into our satellite?"

"She stole a sat truck in Illinois."

"But that still doesn't explain—"

"Look, I don't know!" the engineer said as

he checked connections and wires. "That's what we have to figure out."

"Maybe she really is in Israel and they're tapping in from there."

The engineer shook his head. "She stole the thing in Illinois. You think they floated to Israel?"

"Better call Meninger."

"Yeah, Carl will trace it."

Carl's cell phone beeped. He let the engineer leave a message. "Things are getting hot down here," Carl said to the kids. "We've got one more chance. Let's roll."

"Now?" Mark said. "In the middle of Damosa's speech?"

"Right now."

Vicki took her place and watched Dr. Damosa walk back and forth on the dove stage. "Peace comes with a price, and that price must be paid by those who enjoy it. There are some of you who think what I'm saying doesn't apply to you. You just want the band to come back. That's okay. I want to hear them again too."

Damosa paused for dramatic effect, and the camera zoomed out. It panned the crowd and got tight shots of those in attendance.

"If you want peace, you must commit to it.

You can't *say* you follow the Global Community or that you *like* Potentate Carpathia. You must join us."

Conrad held up a hand, then pointed to Vicki. The screen switched from the stadium to Vicki. "Go!"

"Hi, it's Vicki B. again. Sorry to have to break into Dr. Damosa's speech, but he's making a good point. If you want to be part of something, you've got to do more than just talk about it. That's what I want to challenge you to do right now."

Conrad hit a button, and on the bottom of the screen flashed the kids' Web site, "www.theunderground-online.com."

"I told you earlier how many of the Bible's predictions have come true. If you read Tsion Ben-Judah's words on our Web site, you'll see this isn't some loony guy looking for attention. If you're skeptical, read it."

Vicki stood and leaned against a table. Mark zoomed in tight on Vicki's face. "But many of you know the stuff the Global Community is throwing at you is hollow. You don't have peace with God. Every time something terrible happens—an earthquake, stinging locusts, meteors, whatever—you're scared. You're afraid you might be the next one whose name shows up on the death list.

"I want you to know you don't have to be

scared. You don't have to be afraid that God's going to zap you. You can have real peace with him today.

"Dr. Damosa was right about there being a cost to peace. It cost God the death of his Son, Jesus Christ. Jesus gave his life as a sacrifice for you and me, so that we could be forgiven and made right with God. If you want to commit your life to a peace that will be in your heart and will last not only a lifetime, but even after you die, you should pray with me right now."

Lionel watched people outside the stadium talking and calling for the return of The Four Horsemen. But when Vicki started her message, they became quiet.

"I think this girl is one of the Judah-ites," someone nearby said.

"Shut up," someone else said. "I want to hear this."

Carl watched the control room closely as Vicki continued her prayer. The engineer and others frantically searched the room.

"Where's Meninger?" the engineer screamed.

Carl turned down his monitors and dialed the control room. "I got your message. What's up?"

"Get in here now! Somebody's pirated our signal, and we can't find the source."

"What!?"

"It's the Judah-ites. Instead of the live feed from Jerusalem, we've got some girl praying."

Another phone rang. "It's Damosa!" someone screamed.

"How soon can you get here, Carl?"

Carl noticed Vicki was about to end her prayer. She looked at the camera, smiled, then gave the Web site address again.

"There's no time," Carl said. "Cut the main power grid for the entire facility. That'll cut out the satellite feed, but it'll also cut off the girl. I'll be there as soon as I can."

Lionel heard Vicki's last words before the screen went blank. Sam looked at him and said, "Incredible."

A boy about Sam's age walked up and stared. "Why do you guys have that funny looking thing on your foreheads?"

ELEVEN

Carl's Dilemma

VICKI collapsed in a chair and sighed. Conrad smiled and nodded at her. "Told you."

"What?" Vicki said.

"That you'd be even better live."

Janie ran in. "You were awesome!"

Lenore carried Tolan in and hugged Vicki. "God used you today, young lady. He was bringing people to himself through you."

Vicki wiped sweat from her forehead. "I was really nervous when I thought of all those people watching. Then I remembered my speech teacher. She said I should focus on one person and talk to him. So I pictured somebody sitting there by the camera."

"Who?" Lenore said.

"You don't know him. His name was Ryan Daley. He was one of the original members of the Young Trib Force who died in the wrath of the Lamb earthquake."

After Vicki's transmission had been cut, Lionel and Sam wandered into the stadium to see if they could find any more new believers. When they reached the top of the runway, the lights went out and The Four Horsemen came back onstage. As fire flashed behind the group, Lionel scanned the crowd. Every few rows he saw kids with the mark of the believer. As the music began, many of them made their way out of the stadium.

"Come on," Lionel said. As new believers filed out, Lionel and Sam handed them invitations to General Zimmerman's home. Sam and Lionel split up as more believers left the concert.

"How did you know I'd prayed that prayer?" one girl asked Lionel.

He pointed to his forehead and explained the mark. The girl said she was going right home to look up the Web site of the Young Tribulation Force.

When Sam and Lionel finally got back together, they had both run out of flyers. Sam said he had written the General's address on scraps of paper and even on people's hands. "I lost count at about seventy."

"I talked to around a hundred," Lionel said.

The music still rocked the stadium. Lionel and Sam headed back to give the others the good news.

Vicki wanted to thank Carl for his work, but he didn't answer his phone. The kids gathered to watch a recording of Vicki's message, but Mark interrupted and called everyone upstairs.

Lionel and his friend Sam were on the computer screen when Vicki walked into the room. When they spotted her, they clapped. Judd was in the background giving her a thumbs-up.

"I don't know how you did that, but it was beautiful!" Lionel said. He explained what had happened outside the stadium after her broadcast. "We didn't see any believers beforehand, but we counted almost two hundred coming out of the stadium."

"And think of all the other locations that aired you," Sam said.

"You'd better get ready for a lot of hits on the Web site," Lionel said.

"I'm behind on one of Tsion's letters," Mark said. "If somebody else can handle that, I'll write something for people who prayed today."

"Call it the Vicki B. File," Lionel said.

Vicki smiled. "I'll take a shot at Tsion's letter, if that's okay."

Mark agreed, and Lionel and Sam said good-bye. Judd stepped closer to the camera. "Wish I could have seen you tonight, Vick. Sounds like a pretty good show."

"It was a team effort. What's up with you?"

Judd gave the kids an update on General Zimmerman and Mr. Stein's meetings. "Hopefully a lot of kids who saw the broadcast will come."

"Anything we can pray about?" Conrad said.

Judd hesitated. "There is something. A believer I know is about to get into trouble."

"With the GC?" Conrad said.

"Yeah. And it could put the rest of us in a tight spot. Pray that I'll know what to do when the time comes."

All the kids said they would pray. Tolan toddled into the room and waved at Judd on the camera. Everyone laughed.

Vicki went to her room to read the letter from Tsion Ben-Judah. Vicki loved everything Tsion wrote. This letter dealt with the Global Gala that was coming up quickly. Vicki shook her head. With all the death and grief in the world, Nicolae Carpathia wanted to throw a party.

Tsion said he would not attend the Global Gala, even though he had been invited as an international statesman. *An earthquake is prophesied that will wipe out a tenth of that city,* Tsion had written.

Vicki thought of Judd, Lionel, and the others. Would they be safe from the earthquake? Would other believers be hurt?

Vicki read the rest of the letter and tried to rewrite it in a way anyone could understand. At first it felt weird to change any of the letter. But she knew some kids wouldn't be able to understand all the words.

She wrote:

> *Because death will be in the air in Jerusalem next month, I will not attend this outrage. This festival is an excuse to bring about the evil plans of Satan himself.*
>
> *I will follow the Gala on the Internet or television, like the rest of the world. But I believe this event will begin the second half of the Tribulation, called the Great Tribulation, which will make these days seem relaxing.*
>
> *If you watch the GC newscasts, you know how bad things have become. Crime and sin are beyond control. The food and supplies we need to live on are in short supply because many workers who make and dis-*

tribute them have died. Life is cheap, and our neighbors die every day at the hand of criminals who steal things from them. Many Peacekeepers have died, and the ones left are either overwhelmed with their jobs or are crooks themselves.

Vicki moved through the rest of the letter, highlighting Tsion's belief that evil would become worse and worse.

I urge you to prepare for the day when it is illegal not just to read this Web site or call yourself a believer. One day you will be required to take the terrible mark of the beast on your forehead or your hand in order to buy or sell anything.

Don't make the fatal mistake of thinking you can take that mark and privately believe in Christ. Jesus has made it plain that those who deny him before men, he will deny before God. I will talk more later about why anyone who takes the mark of the beast will not be able to change their minds.

Vicki thought of Lionel and Judd. They had called themselves Christians before the Rapture. Playing church wasn't an option now.

If you have asked God to forgive your sins and have trusted Christ for your salvation, you have the seal of God on your forehead. This mark is also not reversible, so you don't have to be afraid of God turning away from you.

Tsion quoted a verse from Romans and Vicki opened her own Bible. She had read the passage before, but thinking about the current world situation brought tears to her eyes. She read: *If God is for us, who can ever be against us?* Vicki smiled. That verse said it all.

Tsion's letter continued to quote Scripture.

Can anything ever separate us from Christ's love? Does it mean he no longer loves us if we have trouble or calamity, or are persecuted, or are hungry or cold or in danger or threatened with death? No, despite all these things, overwhelming victory is ours through Christ, who loved us.

With the apostle Paul, I am persuaded that neither death, nor life, nor angels, nor principalities, nor powers, nor things present, nor things to come, nor height, nor depth, nor any other creature shall be able to separate us from the love of God, which is in Christ Jesus our Lord.

Vicki closed her eyes. She didn't know whether any of the new believers would understand the word *principalities,* so she cut it, but left the rest in. Tsion closed by urging every believer to give thanks to God for every victory he gives. He ended with *Steadfast in love for you all, your friend, Tsion Ben-Judah.*

Vicki thanked God for those around the world who had watched the satellite broadcast and had become believers. She thanked him for Janie and Melinda, whose lives had radically changed. She prayed for Judd and the situation with his friend, and for Carl in Florida.

When she had finished praying, Vicki felt troubled but couldn't figure out why. A few rooms away Tolan whimpered and cried, and Vicki realized why she felt so uneasy. If the kids had to run, there wouldn't be enough room for everyone in the satellite truck.

Carl Meninger sat in his office in Florida waiting for a call he didn't want to take, and hating himself. He had screamed at the people in the control room and blamed them for something he was secretly responsible for—Vicki's satellite broadcast.

"Don't you realize this could mean my job?" Carl had yelled.

The engineer and the others had looked at the floor while Carl ranted and raved. When Carl was finished, the engineer said, "There's no way they could have done what they did unless they had help on the inside. It could be in New Babylon or Jerusalem or it could be here."

"And who do you suppose it is?" Carl said. "Look around. Who's the mole who helped the Judah-ites?"

No one in the room spoke. Carl finally told them to search "every inch of the compound" to make sure the problem wasn't in-house.

Carl felt isolated from the rest of the Young Trib Force. It had been his decision to go back to the Global Community and work from the inside, but he had had no idea how alone he would feel. There wasn't another believer in the entire compound, and Carl missed talking to Vicki, Mark, and the others.

He read Tsion Ben-Judah's e-mails religiously in his apartment. The rabbi's Web site, along with www.theunderground-online.com, was his lifeline to other believers.

The phone startled Carl. He checked the readout and sighed. His supervisor was a foulmouthed man who could make anyone feel worthless. He picked up the phone, and the man screamed at him. Carl held the phone away from his ear as his boss cursed and threatened Carl if Vicki ever got on the air again.

"I understand, sir," Carl said. "We're working to find out how it happened."

"Work faster," the supervisor said. "I've got Damosa and his people, and even Fortunato, busting my chops."

"I heard Fortunato was traveling," Carl said.

"He is. Called me from Africa or wherever he is this week and said if we didn't find this nest of Judah-ites, he would personally see there would be GC personnel executed."

"Executed?"

"Yeah, so make sure no one's working on the inside. We think we know where this girl and her cohorts are."

"Where?" Carl said.

"Illinois. A Morale Monitor got kidnapped by these crazies. Choppers are looking for a stolen satellite truck."

"Any luck?"

"Not yet, but we'll find them."

"I'm sure you will, sir."

"I want a full report on anything suspicious. Oh, and one more thing."

"Yes?"

"Dr. Damosa has called another satellite school uplink for this Saturday to make up for this fiasco. The Global Gala starts Monday. I don't have to tell you how important it is that this goes as planned."

"Yes, sir," Carl said.

Carl hung up and turned on his cell phone. He had turned it off to make sure no one from the Young Trib Force called him while he was talking to the others. Now he couldn't wait to talk with Vicki and Mark. It was time for an encore.

TWELVE

Saying Good-Bye

WHEN Mark told her what Carl had said, Vicki called a meeting of the Young Trib Force. Everyone crowded into the computer room. Conrad held Tolan to give Lenore a break.

"Marjorie told the GC everything she knows," Vicki said. "We need a twenty-four-hour lookout in the bell tower."

Darrion volunteered for the first shift.

Shelly raised a hand. "Why don't we all just leave? Wouldn't that be safer?"

Mark stood. "Because Damosa's called another satellite meeting for this Saturday."

Vicki nodded. "The reports from around the country and a couple of sites overseas tell us we've had incredible results. The truth is changing these pro-Carpathia kids. We estimate there were one to two hundred decisions made at each site."

"That means there are thousands who are now believers," Charlie said.

Vicki nodded. "We think a lot more might pray at the next meeting. We can't throw away this opportunity."

"What about Carl?" Darrion said. "He's going to get caught."

"They've asked him to head up the transmission this time," Mark said, "so he's wiring a button underneath the control board that will let him switch back and forth without anyone knowing."

"But they'll eventually find it," Darrion said. "And even if they don't, they'll punish him for letting Vicki get on the air again."

Vicki took a deep breath. "You're right. He's in trouble if I go on again, but he wants to take the chance. He thinks this may be our last shot."

"If everything goes as planned," Mark said, "he'll get out after the broadcast."

"What about us?" Janie said. "Where are we going?"

Vicki had thought about that question for weeks. The truth was, she didn't want to leave the schoolhouse. It was the perfect hideout. There was space for the kids to spread out and not bother each other, and they had been able to take in unbelievers.

"There are a few of you who came here during the locust attack," Vicki said. "We'd love to be able to stay together, but we can't. We'd like you to go back to your homes and tell others what you've learned. Help them know God."

Tolan squirmed in Conrad's arms and got down. He went to his mother and hugged her. "Mommy cry?"

Lenore picked him up, tears streaming down her cheeks. "I'd like to say something." She handed Tolan to Shelly. "You kids saved my life. Literally. And you saved my son's life. But that's not the best thing you did for me. You gave me a reason to go on. You showed me how I could know God. For that, I'll be forever thankful.

"I knew this day would come. I didn't want it to, but I figured eventually the GC would find this place and you'd have to run. My house is not big, but I'm willing to open it up to any of you who want to stay with me."

Charlie raised a hand. "Do I get to go, or do you want me to stay here?"

Vicki smiled. "You're with us."

Charlie smiled and slapped Conrad a high five.

When the others had left the room after

the meeting, Darrion shared an idea, and the kids agreed it was a good plan. They helped the others pack and said good-bye. Vicki held Tolan a long time and wiped away a tear. "I wanted to watch you grow up."

Conrad loaded the small car and handed Lenore the keys. "We won't be needing this."

Lenore strapped Tolan in the back and waved. "We'll be praying for you every day."

With the Global Community Gala approaching fast, Judd, Lionel, Sam, and Mr. Stein moved to General Zimmerman's home to be closer to the city.

"I talked with my neighbor today," the General said. "Chaim Rosenzweig is excited about being invited to the Gala as an honored guest."

Judd shook his head. "He still thinks Carpathia is a good guy?"

"Apparently so. I tried to talk with him, but he seemed tired. His speech was somewhat slurred."

"Did you tell him about the earthquake prophecy?"

General Zimmerman nodded. "He wouldn't listen. I tried to explain what happened to me at the meeting, but he said he has many

Judah-ites trying to convince him to become one of them."

"I hope he does before it's too late," Judd said.

Late Friday afternoon Vicki climbed into the bell tower to relieve Janie. Janie gave her a pair of binoculars, scooted to the other side of the small enclosure, and pointed. "They'll come from that direction."

Vicki wiped away a bead of sweat. The intense heat of July and August had given way to a sweltering September. She closed her eyes and thought of her home in Mount Prospect. Her family had lived in a trailer that had only one air conditioner. On hot nights, the family crowded into the cool room or sought refuge in a screened-in porch her father had built. The constant hum of the air conditioner would put the others to sleep, but not Vicki.

"What are you thinking?" Janie said.

Vicki told her and Janie smiled. "At Northside we used to put wet towels over us on nights like this. We only had one fan per floor."

Vicki told Janie she could go, but Janie said she wanted to stay. "I've got a bad feeling I'm going to mess things up."

"What do you mean?" Vicki said.

"I've done a lot of bad stuff. From booze to drugs, stealing to, well, you name it. What happens if I go back to any of that?"

"Do you want to go back?"

Janie cringed. "Never."

Vicki sat back and smiled. "God's working on you."

"What?"

"I know you think I'm some kind of saint, but the truth is, I was pretty messed up myself. I did bad stuff and didn't care, because it was fun. After I came to know God, I wondered if I'd ever go back."

"Did you?"

Vicki shook her head. "I'm not perfect, by any stretch. But after I understood how much God loves me, I didn't want to do any of that. It's like God opened a door. When I saw what was on the other side, I didn't need the booze or hooch or anything else to make me happy."

"Sometimes the stuff I did comes back on me and I think maybe God made a mistake. He couldn't love somebody like me."

"But he does. All I have to do is look at your forehead, Janie. That mark is God's seal that says you're his child."

Janie sat with Vicki and talked until dark. When Mark relieved Vicki a few hours later, Janie was still there.

Carl Meninger made sure no one was in the control room very early Saturday morning when he checked the system a final time. He had asked Conrad and Mark to leave the camera on at the schoolhouse. He punched up the satellite feed and saw a volleyball with a face drawn on it. Underneath someone had written, "Hail, Potentate Nicolae Carpathia."

Carl grinned and tried the button below the console. He raised his knee a few inches and pushed it. No one would be able to tell he was the one allowing the kids to have their say.

It was still dark when Vicki awoke and checked her notes for the broadcast. She couldn't wait to tell more people the truth.

Dr. Damosa walked swiftly to center stage of Teddy Kollek Stadium, beaming in the late-morning sun in Jerusalem. When he spoke, Conrad punched a button on his watch. "We're on in exactly seven minutes."

"How do you know that?" Shelly said.

"Carl's instructions," Conrad said. "He can't communicate by phone, so we're supposed to go on exactly seven minutes after Damosa begins."

Vicki took her place in front of the camera. Dr. Damosa welcomed everyone around the world and in Jerusalem and explained that some would be watching by tape delay. "Only two days from now we will experience the most exciting event in the history of the world. Already more than a million people are here to enjoy Potentate Carpathia's Gala. We will celebrate without limits. Young and old alike are gathering. But you don't have to be here to enjoy the party. You can participate wherever you are."

Damosa paused. "I need to mention something that happened at our last gathering. Someone illegally broke into our satellite signal. This is a criminal offense and will be treated accordingly. We believe the young Judah-ites are the ones responsible, but we have fixed that problem."

The crowd cheered.

"I wish we could go on right now," Vicki said.

"Five minutes," Conrad yelled.

Carl Meninger checked monitors and different audio and video meters. The control room was crowded and getting hot. He asked someone to turn up the air-conditioning.

Carl's boss walked in and surveyed the scene. "Everything all right?"

Carl nodded but kept his eyes on the equipment. "We've checked out every possible way they could get in. There's no chance they'll do it this time."

Carl took a deep breath. He hoped he could get away before the GC arrested him. He glanced at his watch.

Three more minutes.

Vicki sat straight and pulled her hair behind her ears. It had been a long time since she had cared about her looks. Shelly applied Vicki's makeup and said, "Perfect."

Dr. Damosa announced the special musical guests and said they would be performing at the Gala the following week. The crowd cheered again.

"But first, the real reason we are here. We have been talking about your responsibility as citizens of the Global Community. In order to live in peace, you must help us work for peace."

Damosa's speech slowed. The camera focused on the man's eyes, and Vicki felt uneasy. He spoke softly, as if he wanted to put his audience into a trance.

"This is getting weird," Shelly said. "You think he can do what Carpathia did?"

"You mean put people under some kind of spell?" Mark said.

"I wouldn't put it past him to try," Vicki said. "How much time?"

"Two minutes," Conrad said.

"We need to start now. Is there any way to call Carl?"

Carl watched Dr. Damosa and sensed a change in the room. People behind him stopped talking. Damosa's voice was mellow, inviting, and evil.

Carl breathed a prayer for the kids in Illinois. He couldn't let this go on a minute longer. He raised his leg slightly and touched the button underneath the control board.

"You're on," Shelly whispered to Vicki.

Vicki looked up and saw herself on the monitor. She smiled. "Hi, it's Vicki B. again. I know many of you heard about me from the last meeting, but you didn't get to see me, so the Global Community invited me back."

Vicki stood and crossed her arms.

"Actually, that's not true. Right now, there are technical people trying to figure out how we're doing this. I really don't understand it myself, but I do know this. Dr. Damosa and the other GC leaders don't want you to hear what I have to say."

Panic. Chaos. People in the control room went into a frenzy when Vicki came on the screen. Carl's boss grabbed him by the shoulders and shook him. "Get that girl off there!"

Carl glanced at a side monitor and saw Dr. Damosa at Teddy Kollek Stadium. The man glared at the screen behind him and ran off the stage. Seconds later the phone rang.

Carl shouted orders and hit switches on the control board, but nothing worked. Vicki Byrne was on the air.

As Conrad put the kids' Web site address on the screen, Vicki quickly explained the truth about God. Vicki used Janie's life as an example.

"A friend of mine used to buy into the Enigma Babylon One World Faith. She had done some bad stuff in the past and wanted to follow God. But it wasn't until she understood who Jesus was and what he did for her—"

A ringing stopped Vicki midsentence. She tried to concentrate and keep going. Someone ran downstairs and burst through the door. It was Darrion. "They're here! The GC are coming up the driveway!"

Conrad turned off Vicki's microphone. "Let's go."

"No," Vicki said. "Turn my mike back on and get out of here. I have to finish."

Conrad frowned. "Hurry," he whispered as he turned the microphone back on.

The others climbed down to the secret passage that led to safety. Charlie was the last in the group. He looked at his painting, then at Vicki. "I'm not leaving without you."

Vicki checked the monitor. She was still on. She had to finish her message and get out before the GC stormed the schoolhouse.

About the Authors

Jerry B. Jenkins (www.jerryjenkins.com) is the writer of the Left Behind series. He owns the Jerry B. Jenkins Christian Writers Guild, an organization dedicated to mentoring aspiring authors. Former vice president for publishing for the Moody Bible Institute of Chicago, he also served many years as editor of *Moody* magazine and is now Moody's writer-at-large.

His writing has appeared in publications as varied as *Reader's Digest, Parade, Guideposts,* in-flight magazines, and dozens of other periodicals. Jenkins's biographies include books with Billy Graham, Hank Aaron, Bill Gaither, Luis Palau, Walter Payton, Orel Hershiser, and Nolan Ryan, among many others. His books appear regularly on the *New York Times, USA Today, Wall Street Journal,* and *Publishers Weekly* best-seller lists.

Jerry is also the writer of the nationally syndicated sports story comic strip *Gil Thorp,* distributed to newspapers across the United States by Tribune Media Services.

Jerry and his wife, Dianna, live in Colorado and have three grown sons.

Dr. Tim LaHaye (www.timlahaye.com), who conceived the idea of fictionalizing an account of the Rapture and the Tribulation, is a noted author, minister, and nationally recognized speaker on Bible prophecy. He is the founder of both Tim LaHaye Ministries and The PreTrib Research Center. He also recently cofounded the Tim LaHaye School of Prophecy at Liberty University. Presently Dr. LaHaye speaks at many of the major Bible prophecy conferences in the U.S. and Canada, where his current prophecy books are very popular.

Dr. LaHaye holds a doctor of ministry degree from Western Theological Seminary and a doctor of literature degree from Liberty University. For twenty-five years he pastored one of the nation's outstanding churches in San Diego, which grew to three locations. It was during that time that he founded two accredited Christian high schools, a Christian school system of ten schools, and Christian Heritage College.

Dr. LaHaye has written over forty books that have been published in more than thirty languages. He has written books on a wide variety of subjects, such as family life, temperaments, and Bible prophecy. His current fiction works, the Left Behind series, written with Jerry B. Jenkins, continue to appear on the best-seller lists of the Christian Booksellers Association, *Publishers Weekly, Wall Street Journal, USA Today*, and the *New York Times.*

He is the father of four grown children and grandfather of nine. Snow skiing, waterskiing, motorcycling, golfing, vacationing with family, and jogging are among his leisure activities.

Hooked on the exciting
Left Behind: The Kids series?
Then you'll love the dramatic audio!

[illegible]

[illegible]

[illegible]

[illegible]